BURNT HOUSE

BURNT HOUSE

A Novel in Stories

Lowell Mick White

Buffalo Times Press
Austin

Cover: Niko Pirosmani, "Arsenali Mountain at Night"
Interior Photographs: Bollinger of Gassaway
Author Photograph: ABP
Book Design: BTP

Buffalo Times Press is an imprint of **Alamo Bay Press**
Pamela Booton, Director

For orders and information:
Alamo Bay Press
825 W 11th Ste 114
Austin, Texas 78701
pam@alamobaypress.com
www.alamobaypress.com

Publisher's Cataloging-In-Publication Data

(Prepared by The Donohue Group, Inc.)

Names: White, Lowell Mick, 1958-

Title: Burnt house : a novel / by Lowell Mick White.

Description: Austin, Texas : Buffalo Times Press, [2018]

Identifiers: ISBN 9781943306114

Subjects: LCSH: Love--Fiction. | Loss (Psychology)--Fiction. | Betrayal--Fiction. | West Virginia--Fiction. | Appalachian Region--Fiction.

Classification: LCC PS3623.H57865 B87 2018 | DDC 813/.6--dc23

For

Andrea Bates

The road going home was pocked with holes,
That home-going road's always full of holes;
Though we slow down, time's wheel still rolls.
            —Natasha Trethewey

When you tell someone a story, basically you are
passing it along to them, and you make them
responsible for it...The weird thing that happens
is the people who listen to you get their sense of
their own responsibility for this story, to turn it
around and retell it.
            —Larry Heinemann

BURNT HOUSE

Note

There is an actual town called Burnt House in Richie County, West Virginia. When I was growing up I traveled through it many times on my way to and from my grandparents' house in Gilmer County. When I asked about the town's name I was always told that it derived from a tavern that burned down in the early 19th century, leaving behind nothing but a crumbling sooty chimney. For the purposes of these fictions, I've appropriated the name of the town and placed it some thirty miles to the east, along the upper reaches of Leading Creek, in Lewis County. My fictional Burnt House—along with all the people who live in it and the incidents that arise from it—is a product of my imagination and bears no connection to the actual community.

BURNT HOUSE

Part One
Big Snoop in Exile

Exiled

I was always held responsible for my teenaged exile to West Virginia.

I was 12 or 13 when that part of my life started—the years blur—and living in Toledo with my parents, and my mom ordered me to put Dad's clothes in the washing machine. I'd always been taught to check the pockets first, fussed-at way too much when I didn't do it carefully, and so I squeezed the pockets of a pair of chinos. Felt something hard. I pulled it out: a key, a motel key—they had real keys back then, not cards—with a red plastic diamond dangling that said The Maumee Inn.

The Maumee Inn. Yeah. All those years later and it still sounds sleazy.

My mom was in the kitchen. I stuck my head out of the utility room, held up the key and rattled it.

I asked, "What's this?"

My mom turned off the faucet and walked over and took the key from me. Her hands were still wet.

She said, "It's a key."

I said, "Yeah...?"

My parents had been arguing for years, all my life, since before I was born, high school hometown sweethearts who for some reason locked themselves together for life, spending all their time more or less angry, cheating on each other, drinking, fighting—but then that key appeared and made everything worse. A few days after I found the key Dad moved out. Then he moved back in. Then Mom moved out and then back. Then Dad moved out again, and back, and out, and back. Then Mom moved out and back again, and then they both moved out—for good. This all took weeks—months, I guess, now, thinking about it. Screaming and yelling much of all the time, no matter who was moved in or out—screams, threats, blows, things busted. At nights I would stay in my room with my cat, listening to them fight and thinking over and over that this was all their business, their life, their mess. None of it had anything to do with me. I didn't have anything to do with them. I didn't want anything to do with them. Still they tried dragging me into the middle of things—fighting for years, and they decided to blame that key for the bust-up, and they blamed me for finding the key. One time my dad even asked me why I had to show that key to Mom, why I had to rattle that goddamn key around. If I'd just tossed that key in the fucking trash. If I'd just ignored it. If I hadn't been such a goddamn snoop all the time getting into everybody's business. If I'd just forgotten it. He never forgot it. I never forgot it. None of us ever forgot it.

So, when they finally—thankfully—busted up, I got packed off and sent away, exiled to Burnt House, West Virginia, the town where they had grown up. Summers, Easters, Christmases were all in Burnt House. Some school years were spent with Dad, some with Mom, a couple were spent half one place and half another, and one year I went home to Burnt House for Christmas and just decided not to go back to school and nobody even noticed or cared. Everything away from Burnt House was always in flux, confusing and depressing and angry. Exile was far better. I always wanted to get back to Burnt House.

One time I was staying with my mom, who was going to graduate school at Ohio State—I was always riding the stupid bus going from Toledo, where my dad still lived, to Columbus and back again, and then sometimes on to West Virginia—and we were watching TV, watching an old movie version of *Long Day's Journey into Night*, with Katherine Hepburn and Jason Robards. My mom was drinking vodka and getting more and more agitated and exasperated.

"This is ridiculous!" Mom said. "Whoever heard of a family like that?"

In case you've never seen *Long Day's Journey into Night,* it's the story of the messed-up Tyrone family, where mother is a drug addict, dad's an alcoholic, older brother a crazy alcoholic, and the younger brother a sensitive artistic type and probably an alcoholic, too. There's lots of drinking and arguing and soul-searching.

"Whoever heard of a family like that?" Mom asked again. "This is just—it's *yuck.*"

"Mom," I said. Thought. Where was I supposed to begin? Where? With her? With Dad? With Dad's side of the family? Mom's side? Both of them and everybody else too on both sides all had problems of one kind or another. Tragedies. Screw-ups. Cruelties. Crazy things. Stupid things. Bad, bad, sad things that nobody ever forgot, things people never talked about openly but only sometimes related in whispered hinting half-stories after dark.

"Us!" I finally said. "*We're* a family like that!"

"Oh, we are not," Mom said. "You don't know what you're talking about."

Was she blind? Deaf? Drunk? Deliberately stupid?

"Oh, come on," I said.

"You don't know anything," Mom said.

That's what she thought.

I guess that's what she wanted to think. That I was ignorant. That I knew nothing.

But I did know a few things, and I learned a few things more. A lot of things, really. I wasn't much of a talker when I was a kid, I was a reader and a listener. A snoop, too, like my dad said. I wanted to know everybody's business. I read old letters, I went through dusty boxes of photographs. I liked listening to the old timers tell their stories. I listened to all the gossip, and I believed some of it. In the end I knew my family better than any of them knew themselves. For a long time the world outside me was more important than the world inside me, and that was the time in my life when I got to know Burnt House. I learned all the stories in that town. Down Stalnaker Creek from the Stalnaker's house, where I stayed most of the time, then on down Horn Creek to Route 47 and up through the little community, past the little string of houses, past Butchie's store and the church and the schoolhouse, past the collapsed Langford house, past the Ellysons and the Talbots, past the post office and Page's store, then up Hog Run where a few other families lived—past all those houses, all those lives—I knew that place and I knew the people who lived there and I knew their stories better than I've ever known anything else. So, yeah, I knew a lot of things.

But the biggest thing I knew—the biggest thing I knew right then—was not to tell about what I knew.

Telling had to wait.

July 17, 1978

I was 15 that summer and I was living with my grandmother and my Aunt Liza, and one day my father came to Burnt House for a visit, and he brought his new girlfriend, Norma. Norma wasn't the woman he'd been sleeping with when my mom found out he'd been screwing around—when I'd helped my mom find out he'd been screwing around—she was someone he met later, a big blonde woman who taught sixth grade, very cheerful and pleasant toward everyone. Of course I hated her.

We heard the car coming from a long way away. Our house was at the top of a holler back from the county road, which ran up along Horn Creek. Cars had to turn off onto a gravel track that ran up alongside Stalnaker Creek, and then drive directly in the creek bed for the last hundred yards or so, bumping up and down and bottoming out on rocks until they could turn up into the yard, at the house. We were pretty isolated.

I sat on the porch with Gran and Liza and Liza's dog, Mike, and we watched the long, blue Monte Carlo scrape up the creek and around some bushes and past an old, collapsed barn, and up into the yard. Mike stood up and looked at the car. It stopped, and we could hear the engine ticking, the creek running. My father got out and looked up at us, and his hair was a bit longer, and he was wearing a big mustache that would have been cool eight or ten years earlier. Mike barked at him twice.

"Shut up," Dad said. "You damn dumb son-of-a-bitch."

His first words back home. I'm not kidding.

Norma got out of the car, tall, blonde, white teeth flashing. You didn't see many women like Norma in West Virginia.

"Hi, everybody," she said.

We just stared. I stared at her, hating her, and Liza—and Mike, too, probably—stared at her hatefully because I hated her. Gran stared too because she didn't know who this woman was with her son. We just sat there staring at her, gray eyes from Liza and myself, and brown eyes with Gran and Mike.

"It's so pretty here!" Norma acted happy.

Dad came around the car and led the way up onto the porch. He didn't look at me.

"Mom," he said to Gran, his mother. He wasn't really a hugger. "Elizabeth. This is Norma."

"Hi, everybody," Norma said again.

"You didn't bring Jean?" Gran asked.

Jean was my mom.

"Well...." What was Dad supposed to say to that? He'd been divorced from Mom for almost two years. He just glanced at me like it was my fault. Gran was giving him a hard time and he blamed me.

"Jackie!" Norma said to me. "You look good!"

"Yeah." I looked down, and then out at the yard and the creek. Water flowing. Norma was trying. I know that now. She was always trying.

They'd brought some groceries, and Liza slowly got up, sullenly got up, and went into the kitchen to try and put a meal together. She was never much of a cook, unless she was stoned, when she'd pour together two or three different-flavored cake mixes and come up with some sort of gooey mess that tasted wonderful if you were high. She wasn't loaded now, though, but she still went into the kitchen and banged around while Norma stood in the doorway watching helplessly and I sat in the front room with Gran and Dad. I tried to say as little as possible. I just stared at the floor, watched Mike sleeping out on the porch. The creek down there in the distance.

"So, you're doing all right, here." Dad looked at me and then at the floor.

After a silence, Gran said, "She's doing good."

"I suppose you're bored."

"No." After a moment I said again, "No."

How could I be bored? There was always plenty to read, and I could go for walks with Mike in the woods, or walk down to Burnt House, and once a week or so we'd go to town, and in the evenings, if she was around, I could smoke dope with Liza and do jigsaw puzzles and bake weird cakes, and in the mornings I could sit on the porch and drink coffee and look at the world, and no one talked to me when I didn't want to talk, no one yelled at me or told me what to do, and everyone let me alone. I did just what I wanted. How many times in life does that happen? How could I be bored?

"You hear from your mom?" Dad asked. Mom was at summer school that year, finishing up her Master's.

"No," I said again. A lie, but so what.

"She called Saturday," Gran said. "They all talked a long time—I bet they ran up the phone bill."

"She's seeing a shrink," I said.

Dad and Gran stared at me. Speechless. Liza was still banging on something in the kitchen.

"Well," I said, "she is."

Shrink—psychiatrist, psychologist, counselor—I didn't know the difference then. Nobody did. But it was a shocking thing, something to be ashamed of, talking to some stranger about all our business. I'm sure Dad felt as betrayed as I did, and Gran, too. Mom was a traitor.

After a while Liza and Norma called us in to the dining

room for dinner—sausage and gravy, green beans from a can, cornbread from a mix. Basic West Virginia food, food for people doing hard physical labor all day.

"Aw, Elizabeth, this all looks so good," Norma said. "I wish you'd have let me help." Norma was one of those teachers who always want their students to love them. She wanted Liza to love her, and Gran, too. And she wanted me to love her. That was a lot to accomplish on a single afternoon eating sausage up a holler in West Virginia, but Norma tried. I was hard to charm, though, and sat silently.

Dad tried talking to Liza. "When are you going back to college?"

"I don't know," Liza said. "I'll go when I feel like it. Maybe I'll take a class or two over at Glenville in the fall."

"A class or two won't get you a degree."

"Maybe I don't want a degree." Liza got up and stomped back to the kitchen to get a glass of water and bang around. When she came back her face was red, though she wasn't crying.

"Sometimes I think Elizabeth's too smart," Gran said. "That's her problem."

"Too smart or too lazy, one," Dad said.

"I'm not lazy—I just don't want to *do* anything!"

"See?" Dad said to Norma. "See? That's why this place is so goddamn backward. Nobody wants to do anything, and so everything falls apart. You'd have to grow up in this fucking place to believe it."

When Liza was 16 or so, Dad brought her up to Bowling Green so she could live with us and go to a better school. But that didn't last long. Liza got homesick and ran back to Lewis County. Then he tried getting her into college in Ohio—tried a couple of times. But she'd always run back to Burnt House. Dad was still pissed at her. He was always pissed at her.

"Well." Norma was all blond hair and white teeth, trying to make peace. "Everybody has their own pace."

"Goddamn backward pace," Dad said. Coming home always made him mad. "Living up some goddamn holler with fucking paint peeling off the house."

Liza tossed her fork onto her plate and stomped out of the room. When my mom and dad were together and I was little and we all lived in the same house, my dad was always the one to toss something down on the table and stomp off. I'd sit with my mom at the table staring down, and maybe my mom would sigh and say, "*Well.*" But that was all when I was a little kid, and as time went on we'd all eat separately at different times in different rooms. It was easier that way.

Now it was Liza that got up and stalked off, and when she left, the rest of us sat at the table, staring.

"God damn," Dad said. Two words.

"Now, Bill," Gran said. "Be nice."

"You know you let that girl get away with too much."

Dad wouldn't ever let anyone get away with anything, except himself.

Later I sat in the front room looking at the television. Black and white, of course, John Chancellor reading the news. We only got one channel, NBC all the time. Gran sat in her chair watching, too.

After a while she asked, "Is your daddy staying the night?"

"He didn't say anything to me."

Which meant no, I hoped.

"I hate it when people act up and show their asses," Gran said. "Your daddy's like that, and Elizabeth's like that, and your granddad was, too."

Outside Dad and Norma were walking around, he was showing her where he'd grown up. He was always sort of ashamed of West Virginia—a lot of people in Ohio were, whose families had come from West Virginia. I sure got teased when I was in school, and so did a lot of other kids. But our family wasn't too bad off. Both my grandfathers worked in the oil fields for years, good steady work, and whatever their faults—and both those men had many, many faults—they had believed in education, and so we weren't all poor and raggedy like myth would have most West Virginians.

Outside they passed a window. I heard Dad say, "You wouldn't believe how much all this has changed."

Then they came in the back door and I could hear them crossing the kitchen.

"Elizabeth!" Dad sounded mad. "Why the hell won't you mow that yard more often?"

I heard Liza's voice but couldn't make out what she was saying. Dad came on into the front room.

"Mom, you've got two perfectly healthy girls living here, why don't you put them to work? This place is falling apart—get them out there mowing the goddamn grass or something."

Gran shrank back a bit in her chair. Maybe she was kind of afraid of my dad. She said, "Oh, they work in the garden some."

Liza had set out a garden back in the spring, before I'd come, but every tomato, bean, pepper, and onion out there would have died if it hadn't been for me. And I didn't do much, really. Watered a little. Neither of us were much for yard work.

"They can get out there and push a goddamn lawn mower around," Dad said. "They can get off their asses and paint a goddamn porch, too."

Norma was just standing back, watching us. Dad sat on the couch.

"Jackie," he said to me. He had that tone of voice he used when he was pretending to be patient. "Listen, this is a tough time. You've got to help your grandmother."

"Oh, we get by fine," Gran said.

Dad ignored her. "You've got to help her, okay?"

"We don't need anything done," Gran said.

Dad just stared at me.

"I know," I said. "I do lots."

"You've got to do more. You can't wait around for your Aunt Elizabeth to do everything, because she won't do anything—"

"Liza does lots around here!" I wasn't going to let him put Liza down.

Dad looked like he was going to yell at me, but he controlled himself because Norma was standing there and he just glared. That was almost worse, really, than yelling.

"Just try to cooperate," he finally said. His new moustache bristled out, his jaw was stiff. "Help your grandmother."

"I do," I said. I couldn't look at him. I just looked at the floor.

Liza came in then from her bedroom. She'd been listening, of course. It was a small house, you could hear almost everything. Liza stood in the doorway and Dad glared up at her.

Liza asked me, "You about ready?"

Dad looked at me.

"Movies," I said. "They show movies down at the old schoolhouse?"

Dad didn't believe me. He looked at Gran.

"Oh, they've got something going on down there," Gran said. "I don't know what. Mrs. Talbot says they've got people watching shows."

"I came all the way down here to see you," Dad said to me. "Norma came all the way down here."

"Well?" I remember thinking something like, Fuck this. You've seen me. Now you can leave. "So?"

"It's just old movies," Liza said. "Mom, you going to let me drive?"

"No," Gran said, "I don't think you need to."

Liza was 22 but Gran didn't trust her with her car, not any more—there had been too many nights when Liza came home late, or didn't come home at all, and a time or two when the car somehow ended up in a ditch or a creek, or other times when she banged Gran's car into a barn or a tree. And she hit a deer once, too. She'd already totaled four or five cars over the years and damaged others. Gran wasn't going to risk Liza wrecking her cars any more.

Dad was still looking at me. "You're going to go down there and leave us."

Now I looked right back at him. I was pissed. I thought, So? What do you care?

I asked, "Well, yeah?"

Dad just shook his head, disgusted. I got up and followed Liza out the door and across the porch and down into the yard. Mike got up and followed us. Dad and everyone stayed in the house.

"Your dad can be an ass sometimes," Liza said.

I shrugged. He was her brother, she could get away with saying things like that. Even though I was mad at him, even though he really was an ass most of the time, or worse, I couldn't ever think that way about him, at least then.

Dad's car was parked under the big oak tree in the yard, in the thick grass—tall, too, pretty tall, the grass reached up above our ankles and somebody should have mowed it, sure, and the car was deep blue, one of those mid-70s Monte Carlos that were long and wavy like a sad pimp's car. The air was cool outside under the tree in the grass.

Liza was already headed down the driveway to the creek. She turned and looked at me. "Come on!"

"Wait."

I stepped back behind the oak and pulled out my knife. My granddad's knife. I never met him, he died just after I was born, but Gran gave me his knife to remember him by, so I'd have something of his. A black-cased jackknife with two blades, a Barlow knife, and I still have it on my desk as I write this. That day I unfolded the shorter, broader blade and I knelt down and I jabbed the blade into the passenger-side rear tire of Dad's pimp car. And again. Air came softly whispering out and I stood up and stepped away from the car.

"That was real smart," Liza said. "Now he can't leave."

I hadn't thought of that.

I glanced back at the house—everyone was still inside—and then turned to follow Liza. I was still holding the knife in my hand.

"Your dad always likes to complain," Liza said.

"I know." I folded the knife back together and slipped it into my pocket.

"He likes telling people what to do, too."

"Yeah."

"I'm never going to be like that," Liza said. "I'm not going to tell people what to do. And I'm not going to let them tell me what to do, either."

That made some sense to me, of course. Fifteen years old, and I was sick of people telling me what to do—and that's why I loved Burnt House. Gran never told me what to do. Liza never told me what to do.

Outside West Virginia the world was full of bullies.

"I don't want to be that way," Liza said. "What's it worth not being happy all the time?"

We went walking down a path that ran along the creek, past a collapsed barn overgrown with vines, young sycamores on the far side leaning over, dark and cool in the late afternoon. Then we came out of the shade, and Hazlitt's house was on a little rise above the creek, at the end of the gravel road. Mr. Hazlitt was out working in his yard, shirtless in a pair of khaki pants, his big gray-haired belly sticking out. His beagles came out and barked at us—at Mike, mostly—and Mr. Hazlitt looked up from his flowers at us.

"Girls," he said.

Mr. Hazlitt was kind of intimidating. Big bald man with a deep voice and that hairy belly.

"Talked to your dad this afternoon when he was coming in," Mr. Hazlitt said to me. He pulled out a handkerchief and wiped it over his sweaty head. "Is he married to that woman he has with him?"

"I don't know." I made a big shrug.

"Who knows," Liza said. She didn't like Mr. Hazlitt very much, and she wasn't afraid of him, either.

"Well, I was just wondering," Mr. Hazlitt said. He bent back over his flowers and we walked on toward town.

"Everyone thinks they need to know everything," Liza said to me. "Or else they already think they know everything."

At Hazlitt's the road switched up from the creek bed to a gravel graded track, and we walked along. A frog in the middle of the track jumped into the grass by the creek and Mike pounced, an old dog's slow pounce, but he didn't catch the frog.

"Your dad's a strange one," Liza said. "Bringing that Norma with him. Did you talk to her any? When we were in the kitchen, she told me about how she grew up in Michigan. She said she grew up on a farm, and she said she thought it was quiet there in the country, but she was never in a quiet place like West Virginia before, and I said, 'Well, we like it quiet.'"

I said, "I don't know Norma that well."

I didn't want to know her that well.

A light-blue Chevy pickup came around the bend and headed up Horn Creek. Whoever was inside waved at us.

"Actually, I don't like things that quiet," Liza said. And that was true: she generally liked things loud and louder. "But you know what I mean."

It was about two miles to Burnt House. The road ran along the side of the hill, to our right going to town, and to our left wide meadows opened up with Horn Creek running through and sheep or cattle grazing, and woods along the tops of the hills. A car passed us, going down, a little gray Dodge.

"Mary Isenhart," Liza said. "Do you know her? She's crazy. All she does is pray—and I mean *pray*."

We got to the main road and Burnt House. Not much of a town then, and less of one now, I imagine, though I never go back. A few houses strung along between the road and the creek. The old one-room schoolhouse, which had been closed for years. A United Methodist Church, which only held services once a month. A post office. Two stores: Butchie's, which was right across the road from the church and the schoolhouse, and Page's, which was across from the post office. Burnt House was a drab little place, and old, and shabby, and everyone there seemed old and shabby even when they really weren't.

Outside Butchie's there were a pair of gas pumps where he sold Gulf gasoline and a tiny grease pit where he did oil changes. There was dried mud everywhere that had been tracked in by tires and a trash drum full of empty oil cans and broken car parts. That evening Butchie sat on a bench next to the front door, smoking a cigarette.

"Girls," he said. "What's the news?"

"No news," Liza said. "And that's good news."

"Thought I saw Bill drive up your way," Butchie said. Everyone knew everything in Burnt House, or thought they did. "He staying long?"

"Just for the day," Liza said. "Unless he gets a flat tire or something."

Inside the store it was dark and cool and all mixed up—fishing tackle, bobbers and hooks, hung from the ceiling and beams along with small auto parts like clamps and fuses, along with combs, plastic door wedges, toothbrushes, and packets of headache powders. The walls were all a jumble. There was a cooler with milk and eggs and hamburger turning green. Another with beer and soda pop. A door opened into a side room where there was a pool table and a jukebox. I could hear voices from the pool room, the soft click of a ball hitting another ball, and then the Rolling Stones on the jukebox. "Miss You." It was a big song that summer. I didn't miss anybody. I was pretty sure I never would. I got an RC Cola from the cooler and took it over to Butchie's fat wife, Claudie, who stood behind the counter.

"You staying busy?" Claudie asked.

"Not too," I said. I was never a big talker then. I was a listener—a watcher.

In the back room Liza was talking brightly to the boys playing pool. They all sort of looked alike with stringy brown hair and wispy mustaches on their lips. One boy wasn't wearing a shirt, and the other two had their shirts unbuttoned, and all three had flat rippling brown bellies. Skinny young boys, talking to Liza, looking at me. In the back another boy—older, really, a man—was leaning over the table lining up a shot, ignoring us. He had long yellow stringy hair, a real mustache that was sort of reddish, no shirt with the usual flat tanned belly. This was Naked Jackson, Liza's boyfriend—sometimes her boyfriend, sometimes not.

I slunk back against the door.

Naked Jackson missed his shot, and then one of the boys talking to Liza made his way back to the table, shirttails flapping. Naked Jackson came over to us.

"What's going on?" Liza asked.

"Oh, nothing much," Naked said. He looked at me. "Hey, city girl."

I'll be straight about it: Naked Jackson made me nervous. I didn't want to have anything to do with him. He was a Vietnam vet, and sold pot and speed around the county, and maybe did some burglaries too. Broke into cars, stole things. Beat people up. Gran said just looking at him you knew he was headed for the penitentiary. Liza, sometimes she liked him, and sometimes she didn't. Right now she didn't too much.

"We're going over to watch the show," Liza said.

"Well, I'll be around later."

"I bet you will."

A door from the pool room led outside and we went through it, and evening was coming and the air was soft.

Butchie was still sitting on his bench smoking a cigarette and watching traffic on the road.

"That Ace Everett likes you," Liza said. "He's not really afraid of girls."

"Oh, god," I said. Ace Everett was the skinny boy with no shirt. Boy—man, Liza's age, more or less. Though he was much the same as the others: skinny, awkward, stupid.

"No reason why you shouldn't have fun this summer."

"I have fun," I said. Who could have fun with Ace Everett?

We crossed the road to the schoolhouse. Every other week a lady from the county library would come and show a movie—and this was in the days before DVDs or even VCRs. She set up a big film projector and actually ran films through it. We sat in the dark and watched old movies: *Citizen Kane* one week, *The Best Years of Our Lives* the next time, and now *On the Waterfront*. Black and white and old. We sat in the dark and we watched.

We: hardly anybody ever came to the movies, only six or seven people a show, and now, for *On the Waterfront,* not even that. The library lady, who didn't count, since she had to be there. Bess Wiant, the postmistress. Mark Sitton and Brandy Riffle, and Liza and me. Mark Sitton was my cousin on my mom's side, my Aunt Irene's boy, and he'd grown up in Minnesota, and he was spending the summer in Burnt House with our Talbot grandparents— lots of young people came back to West Virginia in the summers then, their parents divorcing and they had no place else to go when school was out—like me, like Mark. Mark was a little older than me, though, about Liza's age. Brandy Riffle was a determined, pensive, brown- haired girl, and Liza was sometimes friends with her and sometimes she wasn't—Liza ran unpredictably hot or cold with a lot of people, most people—and right now Liza was mad at Brandy, so I was mad at Brandy, too, just because Liza was, and since Mark had something going on with Brandy I didn't want to have anything to do with him, either, cousin or not. We sat on opposite sides of the room.

The library lady fiddled with the projector and then the movie started. A gritty big city—and I remembered Gran saying once that a city was no place to raise a boy, and I remembered thinking as the movie started, Why only boys? Why not girls? Cities were probably even worse places for girls to grow up, right?—but, anyway, in the movie these boys were men unloading ships, and it all looked cold and noisy and dirty, and the priest was spooky and creepy all dressed in black, and the blond girl was pretty and sad, and you just knew something bad was going to happen to her in her life, sometime, and there was Marlon Brando with his big, ham-shaped face—and Liza leaned over and whispered, "I bet he's a really good kisser."

Yeah? Well, I guessed so, too.

The library lady turned and looked at us, probably frowning at us, but I couldn't tell because I couldn't see her face. She was just a shadow.

After a while, Liza leaned into me again. "This is boring," she said. "I'll be outside."

She got up and banged noisily into a couple of chairs, and went out. It was still a little light out, soft gray evening light, and I could see across the road to Butchie's when she opened the door. The library lady was probably frowning. Then Liza closed the door, not too loudly.

I watched the movie. Marlon Brando had a problem: whether to rat out his buddies in the mob and lose his job or to stay silent and lose the girl and his soul or whatever. He informed, got beat up, and triumphed in the end. The light went up.

"It's like that everywhere these days," the library lady said. Mark and Brandy were whispering about something and glancing at me.

Outside it was full dark. I could see Ace Everett

playing pool across the road at Butchie's with his shirt off. Mike was sleeping right outside the door of the schoolhouse, and he stood and shook himself. I didn't see Liza anywhere.

Mike followed me across the road. Butchie was still sitting on the bench with a cigarette in his hand.

"Seen Liza?" I asked.

"Oh, she went off," Butchie said. "She went to town with that Naked Jackson."

To town: that could be either Glenville or Weston. Or they might not really have gone to town, they might have just parked out somewhere to smoke dope and what all. I started back down the road to home.

"That show any good?" Butchie asked.

I turned and walked backwards a few steps. "It was about this guy who told on his friends so they came and beat him up."

"That took two whole hours?" Butchie asked.

I turned and walked. Mike followed me. A few people were out sitting on their porches in the dark—Mrs. Alltop, old Mr. Davis, Mr. and Mrs. Summers—and they said hello as we walked by. A car or two went slowly down the road. From everywhere around, from the creek, up in the hills, in the trees, in the sky, sound came down—frogs and crickets and owls—and lightning bugs sparked in the darkness.

I turned and headed up Horn Creek, the cracked asphalt road turning to gravel. The gravel crunching under my feet with every step, every thought. Mike, padding long behind me. Liza off with that Naked Jackson. Dad and Norma on their way back to Ohio. Pigeons circling over the gray dirty buildings in that movie. Mom yelling at Dad one night, I'm going to call my lawyer! And me thinking, She has a lawyer? Another time her yelling, You're oversexed! And me thinking, What? My cat, Jody, that died in the winter. Liza said she'd get me a new kitty. Boys with no shirts playing pool. Liza said that Ace

Everett liked me. "I could have been a contender." Okay. Crickets in the grass, owls in the trees. Frogs everywhere. Lightning bugs. Mike beside me. Liza told me about a boy she liked in college. Before she came home.

A car came around the hill. I could see the headlights reflecting up into the sky before the car itself appeared. I stepped down off the berm with Mike to the edge of the ditch and looked away from the light so my eyes wouldn't hurt. Nothing but friendly darkness out there in that night. Safe and warm and soft.

The car passed. We got back up onto the road and walked. Crunched. Stepped. Thought. Then another car came, the headlights first again, and I looked away. The car stopped this time, and my father was driving.

"Where's your Aunt Elizabeth?" Dad asked.

I shrugged big. "I don't know."

"You don't know."

No, I didn't fucking know. Why did he ask again? He sat there in the car in the dark. Norma was sitting on the passenger side of the car, a blond shadowy blob.

"You don't know," Dad said again.

"No, she went to town or something. I don't know."

I stepped away from the car. Took a half-step crunch up the road.

"Get in," Dad said.

"I'm going back to the house," I said.

"I'll take you back to the house," Dad said. "Get in the damn car."

Well. The Monte Carlo was a two-door, and Dad wasn't getting out to let me in behind him, so I went around to Norma's side. Norma was already getting out.

"You sit up front, honey," she said. "Sit with your dad."

"What about Mike?"

"Oh." Norma looked at Mike, wet and dirty from nosing around in the creek and brush. "I guess he can sit back with me." She pushed up the seat and muddy Mike jumped in back and shook himself.

Dad said, "Jesus Christ."

I sat up front. Dad was wearing a different shirt than he'd been wearing earlier, a clean, light blue shirt, but he was still a little smudgy on his hands and arms from changing the flat tire. Ha!

I shut the door and the overhead light went out.

Dad drove down the road a bit, back toward Burnt House. Then he came to a gate leading down to a hay meadow by the creek, a turn-around spot. Dad made a four-point turn, in and out, forward and backward, forward and backward. Then we were headed back up Horn Creek again.

"I can't believe Elizabeth left you to walk back alone," Dad said.

I was staring silently ahead, at the headlights on the road. Broken pavement, stretches of gravel.

"Jackie," Dad said, and then he paused a long time. I could hear the night sounds coming in through the open windows, the deep crunch of the tires on gravel. In the back seat, Norma was petting Mike.

"Jackie, listen. Norma and I are going to get married."

"Yeah," I said.

"Yeah." There was another long pause, and the car creeped up the road in the dark. "We're getting married, and we're going to make a new family."

I stared ahead at the broken asphalt and gravel road.

"And we'd like you to come live with us."

I didn't have anything to say.

"We'd *love* to have you live with us," Norma said from the back seat.

"Yeah," I said. There wasn't anything else to say. So they were getting married. It wasn't any of my business.

"You won't have to change schools," Dad said. "We're going to get a nice house."

Dad turned the car onto Stalnaker Creek road. Mr. Hazlitt's house was all lit up.

"Say something," Dad said.

"What do you want me to say?"

"Shit," Dad said. The road ran out, and we were driving in the creek bed. "Goddamn West Virginia roads."

"Think it over, Jackie," Norma said.

I said, "Yeah."

We splashed up the creek in the dark. Then the trees opened back away and we pulled up into the yard. Gran had the porch light on.

"We came all the way down here to tell you," Dad said. He looked at me like he expected me to say something.

"Well, you told me."

Dad parked the car by the oak tree.

He didn't say anything. Looking at me. Glaring. He was pissed.

I said, "Okay, then."

I got out of the car and stood in the wet grass. Dad just sat there, angry. Norma pushed the seat forward and clumsily squished out, and Mike jumped out too and disappeared. Norma tried to hug me but I pulled away.

"Think about it," Norma said.

"Okay."

I turned and went up the stairs to the porch. I heard the car door shut when Norma got in, and after a moment the car turned around and headed back down the creek. I went inside. Gran was watching TV, the news. Sports. Some baseball players in a big fight.

"Your daddy go back?" Gran asked.

"Yeah, he went back," I said.

I didn't say, He went home.

I was home.

Rat Trauma

Home was also at the Talbot's house—my mother's parents, Pap and Grammaw Talbot. They lived just up the road from Butchie's store in Burnt House, and though I usually stayed up at Gran's on Horn Creek, I was down at the Talbots about every day or so. One time Liza and I went down there to see my cousin Paul, my oldest cousin, who was visiting while he was home on leave from the army. Liza was 17 or so then, and she thought she liked Paul a lot.

It was December, cool and damp, a week or two before Christmas. Dad and Mom weren't divorced yet and they dropped me off in Burnt House while they took a trip together to argue and do whatever all they did when I wasn't around, and so I spent my Christmas vacation reading and hanging around with Liza. We always got along fine then.

This was when Gran still let Liza drive her car—Liza had only had her license a year or two—and Liza drove carefully the two miles down Horn Creek and she looped around at Page's store and pulled up and parked behind Paul's Camaro, which was parked behind Pap Talbot's black Rambler. The front room of the house was close and overheated—the Talbots, like a lot of old folks, were fond of their fires and kept their houses hot. But we had a fun evening anyway watching TV—Detective Colombo, Peter Falk in his old overcoat—and eating popcorn and listening to Paul tell stories.

Paul was a nice-enough young man, and if they'd gotten together he would have been one of the best boyfriends Liza ever had, though not the smartest by any means. He was in Special Forces, the Green Berets, and he was stationed in Korea, and he'd been to Germany and all over, and he told us all about shooting guns and jumping out of planes. It was pretty exciting: we were a couple of girls who had never even been on an airplane, much less jumped out of one. Liza spent a lot of time just staring at him with her big brown eyes, listening and staring. I was probably staring a lot, too.

So then we ran out of popcorn, and the three of us trooped back to the kitchen to make some more. My grandparents were old-fashioned, and they wouldn't have usually let a guy and a girl go off like that out of the room without a chaperone, which meant that I was the chaperone. I knew Pap was sort of keeping an eye on us all too from where he sat on the couch, around the corner and through the dining room, as much as he could. But Paul and Liza did what they wanted to do anyway. Liza opened the back door to let some cool damp winter December air in, and then Paul lit a joint and he and Liza smoked it, and then Paul brought out a half-pint of Southern Comfort, and they each took a swig of that.

Listen: I had never expected such a thing—never even imagined it. It was 1975 and I was 12 years old and naive, I guess, even for that age and time. I'm sure I stood there goggled-eyed, truly shocked at what they were doing.

I probably thought something like...Darn!

Of course Liza knew I wasn't going to tell on her or anything—I loved Liza.

The dope-smoking and drinking didn't seem to do either of them any harm, though, it just made them more cheerful and giggly—there's a powerful lesson I learned, all the lies grownups told about drugs, in addition to all the lies they told about everything else—and we all made a happy mess of the popcorn popping, deliberately leaving the lid off the pot as an experiment one time, and then accidently spilling a cup or so of un-popped kernels. There was popcorn all over the place.

Now, around that time the Talbots had a rat problem at their house. Not just normal ugly, filthy rats like you see in cities, either; these were big old wood rats, giants the size of a small cat, maybe. Pap Talbot had been telling me that they were catching one or two a day in traps they set up around the property.

So there we were spilling popped and un-popped popcorn all over the floor, and I looked up and saw a hole in the ceiling. A pretty big-looking hole.

I asked, "What's that?"

"That's a rat hole," Paul said. "There's one comes down in here every night."

I backed up a little.

"No way," Liza said.

"Yeah—I've been setting a trap in here for him before I go to bed," Paul said. "But I haven't got 'im yet."

"Heck," Liza said. "If there were wood rats coming in my kitchen at night, I'd wait up and blast one with a shotgun!"

Liza always liked talking big.

Paul stood there waiting a second, thinking. Then he nodded. "You know, I could do that—or do something better."

Then he left the kitchen. Liza and I looked at each other. Shrugged. No idea what he was up to. Liza grabbed a broom and began sweeping up some spilled popcorn. No use feeding the rat.

Then Paul came back in the kitchen carrying his KA-Bar knife. You know what a Bowie knife is? A KA-Bar knife is like that—it's like a sword with a nine- or ten-inch blade.

Paul said all the Green Berets carried them. How he got it past his grandparents that night I don't know—maybe he had it hid under his shirt, or maybe they were used to him marching around the house with a sword. Anyway, he came on into the kitchen and held the knife up and we stepped back—Liza toward the open back door of the house, me toward the dining room.

Paul sat the knife on the counter, and nothing happened then. I relaxed a bit, and Liza relaxed a bit more—she took another hit of the Southern Comfort. We tried popping the corn again, and there was more giggling, and it was nice.

And then—a scrabbling sound up in the ceiling.

We all looked up.

"It's that damn rat," Liza whispered.

"Oh...." I said softly, almost a moan. I stepped back again.

Scrabbling. Scrabble-scrabble.

Something in the ceiling right above our heads.

Paul slowly picked up the knife and held it motionless right beneath the rat hole. Squinting. Kind of smiling.

Liza looked at me. It was a small kitchen, but I managed to edge back a bit more against the sink. Liza stood near the open door. Paul was between us with the giant knife.

Scrabbling.

And then—a whisker? I thought so. I thought I saw the rat. Liza later wasn't so sure she saw anything at first. But there was something there. Paul lunged up and then there was a jet of something—blood!

Ah! I screamed.

AHHHHH! Liza really screamed.

Paul jumped back, a big brown squirming something rat rat rat rat rat wriggling fighting bleeding on the end of the blade.

I ran screaming out of the kitchen—Liza ran screaming out the back door. Screaming! Screaming! In the dining room I banged into Pap Talbot, who was coming in all excited by the screaming and he held me up.

"Here now!" he said. That's what old people always used to say when young people were acting up. Here now! "Here now! What's all this?"

"A rat-a rat-a rat!"

Liza burst in then through the front door screaming and breathless and frenzied, and Pap Talbot dropped me and went on back to the kitchen.

"Jesus Christ!" I heard him yell. *JAY-ZUS CAW-RYEST*. "What the hell are you a-doing back here?"

We left just after that. We bolted. We snatched up our coats and left. Ran out that door. Grammaw Talbot was already on the phone to Gran telling her we were on our way—and since it was a party line, half the people in the county knew something weird had happened.

I couldn't calm down. I was gasping for breath—all that screaming! But we ran back out to the car and got in, and then Liza found she still had the half-pint of Southern Comfort in her hip pocket. Still a couple of gulps left. She tossed it to me.

"Hold this."

"Did-you-see-that—" I asked.

"I don't even want to talk about it!" Liza turned the ignition and the car started.

"Oh-my-gosh!"

Pap Talbot came out on the front porch of the house to see us off and he stood beneath the light and waved at us. Waved at us to come back, I think. We drove away. I don't know where Paul was—maybe he was still back in the kitchen wrestling with the rat. Killing it, Green Beret-style, with that sort-of smile on his face.

I caught my breath. I said, "Did you see it?"

"That damn rat!" Liza said. "I don't ever want to talk about it!"

We were passing Butchie's store, and Liza took the bottle from me and finished it off. She rolled down the window—manual windows, then, and the car lurched from side to side as she rolled—and she tossed the bottle. I heard it tinkle on the road behind us.

"I don't believe it!"

"Did you see it?"

"That rat!"

Liza almost missed the turn onto the road up Horn Creek and she skidded some on the gravel. She sped up the road in the dark, fast and faster.

"Oh my god—that rat! It was on the knife—!"

"I know!" I yelled. "Did you see it?"

"I don't ever want to talk about it!" Liza was yelling too. "I don't ever want to talk about it!"

—and then she swerved for something, something or nothing, she swerved and the car went barreling through a fence and banged off the corner of Emerson's barn and then went bouncing bounding rolling smack into the creek. Totaled the car. We were okay, though, more or less—well, in the long run I guess we were okay.

The next day—the next evening, we slept most of the next day—Gran piled the guilt on Liza. How could she do such a thing? Why would she do such a thing? Did she know what people were saying? This went on and on, it seemed like, forever. All why, why, why, and what the neighbors would think. Liza took it for the longest time. She kept her mouth shut and her arms folded across her chest and looked at the floor and shook her head—no, no, no. No.

Nobody once asked me how I was doing.

We weren't wearing seatbelts. Who wore seatbelts?

So. I had a bump on my forehead from where I hit the windshield and a nasty bruise across my shoulder and chest from banging against the dashboard and the door, and I somehow managed to cut my hand on an old bottle in the creek when I fell out of the car.

Nobody cared about any of that.

When my dad called, all he worried about was what

the neighbors were thinking.

"Do you know how much you embarrassed us?"

"I didn't do anything!" I said. "I was just riding—"

"That doesn't matter, goddamn it!"

"My head hurts," I said.

"Your ass is going to hurt, too, if I ever catch you in another car with your Aunt Elizabeth."

When I got off the phone, I took a couple of aspirins and went and sat in a corner. Gran was still going after Liza—Why would you do such a thing? Don't you care what people think? Don't you know how much a new car is going to cost? What were you thinking?

My head hurt, my arm hurt, my chest hurt, my hand hurt. Nobody cared.

Gran said, "I just don't know why you'd ever want to do a thing like that."

Liza stopped looking at the floor and shaking her head. She looked up. Eyes hard. She said, "Mother—"

"Why would you—"

"Mother!" Liza spoke sharp this time.

Gran stopped talking and stared back at her.

"Mother," Liza said, "I was *traumatized.*"

And so that was the first car Liza wrecked.

Pecker on a String

This also happened back in 1978. I wasn't there to see it all happen, but I heard all about it later from people who knew what they were talking about and I think it's mostly true—

So.

Butchie Randolph would sit out there in front of his store that summer, and he'd see those Stalnaker girls walk by every day, two or three times a day, long brown slim legs in their shorts walking up and down the road and back again. They were all of an age, too young, and Butchie knew they were too young, even the older one was too young, but he could still look at them and think. And what was wrong with that?

They could walk, and he could think. That was fair.

There was one soft evening after the younger Stalnaker girl had headed down the road alone in the dark with her dog, and Butchie was sitting out there on his bench, smoking, listening to the night sounds and the occasional click of pool balls inside on the table. Sitting and thinking and smoking. After a while Claudie came out and sat with him.

"You're sure you're going to be able to close up by yourself?" Claudie asked.

"Oh, I reckon."

"If you're not too lazy."

"Oh, now," Butchie said. "Claudie. You don't want to talk like that."

"Well," Claudie said. She finished her cigarette and dropped it to the concrete and stepped on the butt, ground it into the dry, caked mud on the concrete. "Well, I expect I'll get ready for bed, then."

"I'll be along," Butchie said.

Claudie got up heavily and went walking up the road to their house—it was just across and up a bit, next to the church, a neat little house with green aluminum siding and a white picket fence around the front yard that sagged a bit on the downstream side after someone backed a car into it. Claudie walked slowly into the shadows, round all over like an apple—big round head with short stiff black hair, round lumpy shoulders, great big round ass. There was a joke people told about a couple who went to church one Sunday, and when the service was over, the man said to his wife, "Let's go, Crisco," and the preacher asked the woman, "Why'd he call you Crisco?" And the woman said, "Oh, he just calls me that in public, at home he calls me lard-ass." And Butchie watched Claudie walk off across the road into the dark, into the shadows, and he thought, That's my lard-ass all over. Good old lard-ass. Crisco. He couldn't remember the last time he'd seen her naked, didn't want to remember, really, didn't even want to try, it was too much like work, though they slept in the same bed next to each other every night and almost every night Claudie would roll back into him, bump her big round soft lardy ass into him and all, and things would happen. He just kept his eyes shut, thought about other things.

It was funny. Sometimes you'd hear men complain about how their wives wouldn't put out—once a week, once a month, never. And here old lard-ass Claudie wanted it about every night and sometimes more. Pretty good screwing, but you could sink right into her and disappear, if you weren't careful, she was so fat.

That night, though, after the last of the boys finished playing pool and bought six-packs of Stroh's to take home, Butchie shut out the lights in the store and locked up and stepped outside. Burnt House was quiet, houses dark, hills darker rising up, night noises closing in. He looked across the road at his house—dark there too, Claudie hadn't left the light on for him again, though probably she was waiting up in the shadows like a hay mow under the blankets. Well. She'd just have to wait. Butchie went over and got in his pickup and started it and drove on out of Burnt House, past the dark houses and he turned up Horn Creek and on in the night, up over the hill and back down Bloody Run.

When he'd been in the service, in the army, there'd been this training called "low crawl" and it was pretty much that: the men would all crouch over low and get down and crawl through the mud under barb wire like lizards while the drill sergeant yelled and fussed, and maybe some other poor fool would be firing a gun over their heads—and though that was a long time ago, and Butchie was now all fat and middle-aged, he remembered the concept: getting down low to crawl while somebody fussed at you. That was his whole marriage, he thought: Claudie, the drill sergeant, the enemy machine gun fussing and firing while he tried so hard to keep his ass down and out of the way. Poor Claudie, that big old soft pile in the dark next to him in bed, smelling of Ivory dish soap, gazing at him gloomily all damn day through her thick round glasses, never happy about much of anything. Then wanting him to climb up on top of her at night. That was just how it was. What more could a man do? Nothing. Not much, anyway. Not at least on some nights, anyway, nights when after he closed up the store, Butchie would find himself crouched low crawling through the brush in a holler off Bloody Run, low crawling until he came out on an opening just above a little house—Milkshake's house.

Milkshake. Milkshake. Butchie thought, In public I call her Milkshake, at home I call her Tits. He knew her—a hippie-ish woman, though older than some, with traces of gray at her temples, and vast giant wobbly jello-y tits that never saw the inside of a bra—floppy whoppers, each big enough to fund a dairy. When she'd come in to the store—and she didn't come too often—to get a few things, everyone would stop and stare, though Claudie would smile at her kindly, friendly for once, for some reason. Milkshake's real name was Maggie, and she taught art or something like that at the college in Glenville, and she lived in that little house off Bloody Run, and she never closed her curtains.

That night Milkshake's house was all lit up—lights on her porch, by her garage, and in the kitchen and front room. Milkshake herself was stretched out on a couch, her big half-collie half-shepherd half-something dog next to her, her feet up on a low table. Watching TV, maybe—probably, because there was a pale blue light shining back at her. Through his binoculars Butchie saw the light move on her face, her fat chest rising and falling, and rising.

Not too much going on. Butchie lowered the binoculars and shifted, the sweet smell of clover in the air, a screech owl back on the hill behind him, a flash or two of lightning bugs. Crickets and frogs. Not too much going on, just Milkshake watching TV, not even getting ready for bed. Nothing going on, really, just the world.

Then, after a while, a car came around the bend, and slowed, and turned into Milkshake's driveway, and Butchie shrank back into the brush to hide from the headlights. But the light missed him and the car came to a stop in front of Milkshake's garage, and Butchie saw it was a brown-and-white patrol car with a star on its side—sheriff's office. Butchie raised the binoculars: Doy Caldwell, a deputy. He lived over in Glenville. New man—Butchie didn't know him very well. He came into the store a time or two to get a soda pop or something, and he'd smile—a younger man, in his thirties, square-faced, hair nicely parted, polite. Everybody paid attention when he came in the store. Claudie, who watched everybody—everybody—watched Deputy Doy with light flashing off her glasses, the boys playing pool kept playing pool, but they also kept an eye or an eye and a half on Doy—people just watched him, wary, and waited for him to leave. And when he left, someone would say, "Well, he's going somewhere," and everyone else would nod like everyone always did, like they all knew something important, and everyone would wonder who it was getting served or arrested, though nobody knew anything for sure. Nobody knew anything, really. They'd just nod like they did. But now in the night at Milkshake's house, Doy got out of his car carrying a brown paper bag and stood there under the garage light. Inside the house, the big dog jumped off the couch and began barking. Milkshake got up, too, her tits wobbling in her shirt, and she went out onto the porch, and Doy crossed the yard and went up the steps and they kissed right under the porch light, the dog jumping around, happy, and they all went inside. Milkshake took the bag into the kitchen and sat it on a table and pulled out a six-pack of beer—Hey, Butchie thought, he didn't buy that at my store—Stroh's, it looked like, that bronze-and-black can, and she pulled a can from the plastic ring and went back out to the front. The five remaining cans sat on the table.

Butchie thought, Need to put that in the refrigerator.

In the front, Doy took off his gun belt and draped it over the back of a chair, careless. Milkshake brought him the can of beer and he took it and took her, too, pulled her close and they kissed—but the big dog was jumping up between them. Milkshake pushed the dog down, but he jumped up again. Milkshake kissed Doy quickly, then took the dog by his collar and dragged him to the kitchen and shut the door. The dog stood on his hind legs scratching at the door.

Down there between Butchie's legs the horse woke up—twitched, stirred.

Oh—that horse, his pecker.

It moved. All his life. It always did. Back when he was a boy in school, Butchie liked to pull his pecker out and wave it at the girls—oh, they'd squeal and run off. It was fun—it was funny. He'd point the horsey head at them and they'd scream and run away. And the teacher, Rence Talbot, a skinny man with cheerful happy blue eyes behind glasses, a joker with all the other children, they all thought the world of him, 15 or 16 of them first grade through sixth, crammed together in that little schoolhouse in the back of nowhere, up some holler off of Indian Fork at the bottom of Lewis County—the teacher, Mr. Talbot, he'd swat Butchie with a switch and tell him to stop sticking his pecker out. But then Butchie'd pull out his pecker again anyway just to hear the girls scream, and they'd scream and run, and Mr. Talbot would switch him again, but Butchie wouldn't stop, and they went through this over and over, until Mr. Talbot started taking Butchie out behind the school and hitting him with a big stick, a length of broom handle, beat him hard, told him not to stick his pecker out anymore.

But what the hell, Butchie thought now, years later. When you have a pecker like that, a real horse, you have to stick it out, right? It's something to be proud of. You've got to do something with it, even just stick it out and flop it around and show it off if you're too young to do anything else with it. Down below in the house Milkshake and Doy were just sitting on the couch. Talking, probably. Butchie thought they ought to hurry up and get busy, and he squeezed himself again.

Yep. Still there, waking up.

And then there was one day Mr. Talbot took Butchie out behind the school but he didn't bring his stick along. He didn't beat Butchie, he just pulled Butchie's pants down and stared at his naked horse. Looked at it close.

"Well, now," Mr. Talbot said. "That is a pretty good pecker you've got there."

Butchie stood there looking around. Everyone else was back inside the school.

"But we ought to dress it up a bit, don't you think?"

Butchie didn't say anything. He just looked away. There was a ragged cornfield behind the school, a hill beyond that, trees. Woods. Freedom. He could run naked out there and let the horse flop around out in the open air and nobody'd know.

Then Talbot pulled out a length of string and tied it around Butchie's pecker. Put a nice bow on it, like tying a shoelace.

"There," Talbot said. "Now, that'll remind you not to wave your pecker at the girls."

The string wasn't too tight, but he could feel it.

"I don't want you to ever take that off," the teacher said. "Until I cut it off."

Butchie always remembered thinking—Oh.

At recess though he did stick it out again, he had to, stick the horse right out, the collar of white twine bowed and dangling. But this time the girls didn't scream and run. They stared at his pecker curiously, stared, and then one of them said, "You've got a string around your thing!" And they all laughed and pointed, and Butchie stood there on the schoolyard not knowing what to do until he finally pulled the horse back in the barn and buttoned up the door. The girls were still laughing. He looked up and Mr. Talbot was standing there, nodding.

"I said, that was a reminder."

But the teacher wasn't through. Butchie wasn't ever much of a student, he liked talking and cutting up. The next week after the bow, the teacher moved Butchie's desk to the front of the room, stared at him all morning with those happy blue eyes, and then in the afternoon he took Butchie out back and made Butchie drop his pants.

"That string's gone," Mr. Talbot said.

"Slipped off," Butchie said. "They made me take a bath, and I couldn't tie it back. It was all wet."

"Not likely," Mr. Talbot said.

"That water was cold," Butchie said.

This time Mr. Talbot didn't have a string with him—he was holding a length of shiny red quarter-inch ribbon. Mr. Talbot looped the ribbon, stiff and sharp-edged, around the bottom of the horse, the base, and around the horse's soft sloping sides, and he tied it off with a big floppy bow.

Mr. Talbot was a man who sure knew how to tie a knot.

"Now, that's pretty." Mr. Talbot was on his knees in front of the horse like he was going to kiss it, but he didn't. He was just admiring that bow—that horse. His handiwork. "Yep, that's a pretty pecker."

Mr. Talbot got to his feet. Butchie looked past him at the woods—leaves coming down now, in the fall, but still there'd be safety and freedom running in those leaves.

"You see, Butchie, I just want your attention." Mr. Talbot stood there with his hand on Butchie's head. "You understand that?"

"Yes—"

Oh—Mr. Talbot had his attention, all right. That red ribbon, stiff and sharp, it was a harness on the horse—a little bridle—a little halter. All you had to do was yank on it, Butchie thought then, thought forever, you could just yank on it and get my attention quick. It was that way always, yank on my horse, get my attention. Always. Pull on my pecker. Lead my horse. That was true for old Mr. Talbot and for Claudie and for everyone else—pull on my pecker, get my attention.

Sitting there now in the dark, Butchie gave the old horse one more squeeze, and then picked up the binoculars. Focused.

In the front room they were kissing again. Doy pulled Milkshake over to the couch and they fell onto it and Butchie felt tight all over, breathless, and the horse was up now and ready to come out of the barn, and he tried to breathe and inside the house Doy and Milkshake had their heads together not kissing but maybe talking and Doy ran a hand over Milkshake's shoulder and down her chest and then—yes!—he squeezed that big fat soft white tit and they were kissing again and pulling their clothes off—some of their clothes, Doy's pants and then Milkshake's shirt and her boobs all shaking around with her nipples as big as the palm of Butchie's hands, big as a horse's hoof, Doy's head stuck between them and then Milkshake slipped out of her shorts and she settled down on Doy and slid on him right there and they were both shaking and flopping and Butchie saw something moving to the side—and there was the big hairy dog in the kitchen going crazy, careening around knocking over the trash and chewing up bits of paper—and then back in the front room Milkshake and Doy were going slower, slower.

"Damn, that was quick," Butchie said, gasped.

The horse was only barely sticking his head out of the barn.

He looked through the binoculars to see what would happen next—they'd be doing it again, sure. But they were just leaning on in to each other now—Milkshake shuddering, breathing deeply, her tits crushed down against Doy. In the next room the big dog was still jumping around, active, though not as frenzied as before. He scratched at the back door like he wanted out, then at the door to the front room, and then at the back door again. Those five cans of Stroh's still sitting getting warm on the table.

In the front room, Milkshake pulled herself off Doy— bent over and kissed him, tits all wobbly—and then she pulled her shorts back on. Doy lay back on the couch, shirt on, pants off. Butchie focused and refocused the binoculars but couldn't see any sign of Doy's pecker, not anywhere.

Milkshake went into the kitchen. The happy dog

jumped up at her but she pushed him back down and smacked him and pointed at the overturned trash and smacked him again. The big dog slunk back and stood by the back door. Milkshake went over and let him out.

That dog, Butchie thought.

The dog came around the side of the house and pissed on some shadowy bushes, then it made another stop, and then it wandered down to the edge of the creek, right across from Butchie.

"Now, dog," Butchie whispered. "Don't, now. Be still."

The dog froze. Stood there hulked for the longest time in the light from the porch and the garage. He couldn't have heard me, Butchie thought. But he knows something.

The dog coughed. Then barked.

The hell, Butchie thought. He began trying to quietly crawl up the hill, backwards.

The dog broke out in a frenzy of barking and snarling. But he stayed up there in the yard, on the other side of the creek.

Milkshake came out on the porch—still no shirt, but Butchie didn't care now.

"Grip! Quiet, there!" Milkshake shouted.

The dog kept barking.

"Somebody's out there." Milkshake's voice carried across the creek—across the barking of the big dog.

That was enough. Butchie fastened his pants and turned and scrambled up the hill in the dark, grasping hard at greenbriers and filth and pulling up, up—feet slipping. Then the dog took off after him—Butchie could hear it splash across the creek, tags jingling.

Then Doy's voice. "Stop! You, stop!"

Then a pistol shot. Pop! Loud, though, in the night.

Goddamn. Holy hell. Butchie knew nobody could aim a pistol and hit him at night at that range—hit him on purpose, that is—but still, the lawman might get lucky. The hell! He kept scrambling up the hill in the dark, sliding back down, scrambling some more, binoculars hanging from his neck catching on branches, pulling back. Goddamn!

Another shot. Pop!

Butchie heard the dog's tags jangling and jangling closer and closer. Goddamn. Briars tore at his clothes, slowed him, hands all ripped, the dog coming—another shot!—and then Butchie's feet slipped out again, rocks rolling back down the hill, and he slammed face-down into the brush, and then the dog was on him, snarling—trying to sink his damn teeth in Butchie's ass then grabbing his pants leg—

"God damn!"

Then someone else was there—a shape rose up, kicked at the dog. The dog held on to Butchie's cuff, shaking his head.

"Got out of here!" the shape yelled—and Butchie kicked once more at the dog. The dog jumped back, barked three times, and disappeared. Down at the house, Doy was shouting something.

The shape asked, "Got you good, did he?"

Butchie pushed himself to his knees and looked up toward the dark shape. But not a stranger, though—it was Gerald Stalnaker, older brother—a lot older—to that Elizabeth Stalnaker, uncle to that Jackie. Butchie just gaped at him in the dark.

"That girl sure put on a show tonight," Gerald said.

"Holy hell," Butchie said. Gasped.

"We better go before they come looking for us."

Gerald helped Butchie up and then started off around the side of the hill. Butchie followed slowly, his ass hurting—his face and hands, too. Soon they came to a trail of sorts, running beneath dark trees, and the going was easier. Up a little, then down around the head of a holler, and they came to a little cabin perched on the side of the hill, high enough to see Highway 47 below, and off down Alice Road.

"This was that old Smithson place," Butchie said.

"Still is," Gerald said. "My mom's a Smithson."

Butchie followed him up the steps. Moths fluttered around the dim porchlight. A gray striped cat sat on the porch banister watching them. Gerald scratched the cat's head. He said, "Nothing wrong with a little pussy."

Butchie didn't say anything.

"Man, you're a mess," Gerald said. "Go inside and get cleaned up."

Inside the cabin everything was falling apart. A couch listing with a broken leg, dishes in the sink, an old TV with rabbit ears that probably couldn't get any channels, a pair of tattered chairs. A green-covered bible on a shelf next to a rusted Folger's can. Gerald could afford to fix this place up better, if he'd wanted—he lived in Weston and sold cars for a living. Married well, too. Butchie went on into the bathroom and splashed some water on his face from a pan nestled in the sink. Stung like hell. No towels.

Outside Gerald sat at the top of the steps with the striped cat.

"Well," Butchie asked. "I guess I know something about you, now."

Gerald laughed. "Yeah, and I know something about you, too. You're not the only one that likes a good show."

Butchie sat heavily on the steps. The striped cat rubbed her head against his elbow.

Gerald said, "That deputy's been driving up and down the road a couple of times."

"Damn," Butchie said. "He'll see my truck."

"So he sees your truck." Gerald shrugged. "He won't know anything for sure."

Butchie said, "He'll have a pretty damn good idea."

They sat on the porch with the cat. Butchie started worrying about getting home. He could walk back—it was only a couple of miles, maybe three. But what about the truck? And what if the law found him walking on the road? And what would Claudie say, him coming home all scratched up and scarred with a dog bite on his ass? What would he say to people at the store? He could tell people he fell down in the woods. That made a lot of sense. Sure. Fell down in the woods. At night. At night.

"Here he comes again," Gerald said.

Butchie watched the headlights of the deputy's car creep down the road around the side of the hill. Slowly, slowly. Doy had a spotlight mounted on the drivers' side door of the car, and the beam shot back and forth through the woods, then glaring down into the meadow. Doy slowly drove on.

"Maybe she's in the car with him," Gerald said. "Maybe they'll do it in the car."

"Maybe," Butchie said. "I had that girl in a car once."

Then he shut his mouth.

Probably shouldn't have let that come out.

Gerald asked, "What?"

Butchie shook his head. That time with Milkshake. Tits. Her car was broke down coming back from Glenville, Butchie gave her a ride home. They talked for a long time, for the longest time, flirted. Laughed. Told stories. He dared her to tug on the horse—she thought that was funny, and she tugged, and the truck windows fogged all up quick and one of her big white boobs flopped out of her shirt, and the light at the front of her garage glittered in her eyes, glinted off her teeth when she smiled. They never did go inside.

Gerald pushed the striped cat down the steps and scooted over next to Butchie. The cat turned and looked at them angrily.

"Oh, man," Gerald said. "You've got to tell me all about that girl!"

"It was nothing, really," Butchie said.

"No."

Butchie watched Doy's car disappear around the bend. He could feel Gerald next to him—could smell Gerald's body, all the sweat he carried and the smell of grass and clover and cigarette smoke heavy and full in the night air. Butchie stared straight ahead down at the empty road. Then he felt Gerald touch him—touch his leg, his thigh, slowly, then his hand at the barn door, and Butchie closed his eyes and took a deep breath, smelling Gerald again, the horse standing up in his stall—Oh, yes, he thought. All right, then. Pull.

Tater Rumbler

Just up the creek from the Stalnaker house and across a bit was a spot where the water ran a little deeper along a stone outcropping under a vast bark-flaked sycamore, and there was a flat shelf of slate all mossy and soft and quiet next to the water, and that's where I spent most of my time, reading.

When I was a kid I listened more than I talked, and I read more than I listened. For a long time I liked big 19th-century books—books like *Middlemarch* and *Pride and Prejudice* and *War and Peace* and *The Possessed*, books that contained big but comforting and interesting worlds you could enter into and live in for a week or two at a time. I was such a weird, crazy kid. I didn't want to be told what to do—that part of my behavior, of course, was pretty normal—but more than that, I wanted to enter the other worlds of those big books, and I wanted to be left alone, really *really* alone. And at Burnt House everyone left me alone.

There was one Sunday afternoon when I couldn't go off to my rock ledge to read, for it was raining, a steady, all-day rain. That was fine, though—it has to rain sometimes. So I carried my old musty copy of *War and Peace* out to the porch and I curled up on the swing and I read. It was a Constance Garnett translation my mother had given me, a book she said she'd read as a teenager, so maybe Tolstoy was a family tradition or something. That day I lay there in the porch swing and read about Natasha and Sonya, and how their lives were like mine, and how their lives were different. Gran came out on the porch, too, and she was reading one of those detective novels she liked. The rain came down steadily, sometimes harder than other times, and thunder sometimes rumbled.

Then the phone rang.

Liza was inside, sleeping or sulking or something, and she got up and answered it. After a moment or two, she called out, "Jackie! It's your mom!"

Great, I thought. What did she want?

Gran glanced up at me, and then back at her book. I looked out and there was muddy water in the creek.

I went inside. Liza left the phone laying on the stand next to Gran's chair. I picked it up.

"Yeah?" I asked.

I guess Mom started out normal enough—she asked how I was getting along, she asked how the weather was, the usual.

Then she asked, "Aren't you bored?"

Dad asked that, too.

Why were they always asking me if I was bored? Why did they always assume I was bored?

"I'm reading *War and Peace*," I said. I figured she might like that and get off my back. She gave me the book, after all.

But she didn't even want to talk about the book. She said, "There's nothing for you to do there."

"That's okay," I said. Shrugged. "I don't want to do anything."

Outside it was raining hard again—the rain was beating down on the tin roof, the best sound in the world. Inside, the clock ticked. On the wall were framed pictures of granddad, my father, Liza, their brother Gerald, my cousin Danny Bob, and me.

"Honey," Mom said. She paused. I waited. When she said "Honey" like that I always knew she was going to want me to do something I didn't want to do. I knew she was going to boss me around. She asked, "Why don't you come live with me?"

"Because," I said. Of course that's what I said.

"Why?" she asked.

"I don't know."

Our phone was on a party line. I thought about all the people listening in to my business. Our business. My business. Not only was she asking questions that she didn't have a right to ask, she was doing it in public.

Really, I thought, she had nothing to do with me. She didn't deserve to have anything to do with me.

Mom said, "But that doesn't make any sense."

"So?"

There was a pause. I looked at one of the pictures on the wall—my mother and father, years before I was born, smiling, standing out in the yard in front of the house. They looked relaxed and cheerful and happy. That sure hadn't lasted long.

"Jackie," Mom said, "don't be that way. Tell me why you don't want to come live up here with me."

"Because I like it here," I said.

"Because you *like* it there," she said. Mocking.

Right. I liked it there. Because in Burnt House no one ever yelled at me. Because no one ever told me what to do. Because no one ever asked me weird questions, or blamed me for things, or made me feel guilty or bad. Though I didn't know how to say any of that—then, I didn't.

I said, "Because I fit in here."

"Oh, Jackie." Now her voice got hard. "You—you really ought to be ashamed of yourself. When I think of how hard your dad fought to get out of that place, and how hard I fought to get out of there...."

"Oh, shut up," I said.

"You don't really know what it's like—"

"Shut *up*," I said again. I put the phone down sharply—I didn't slam it, I hung up sharply. She'd call back sometime. She was a talker. She thought I didn't know anything so she was going to have to tell me everything. I couldn't stand that. On the wall above the phone that picture of young dad and young mom smiled out at me. They were the ones who didn't know anything. I still don't know if they ever learned anything.

I went back out on the porch.

"Well," Gran said. She didn't ask about my mom. It sometimes occurred to me that maybe she didn't like my mom too much. She said, "Well, it's still raining."

"Really," I said. I lay back on the swing, rocking.

Gran said, "The old-timers would call a rain like this a tater rumbler."

"Yeah?"

"That's right," Gran said. "It's the kind of rain that makes little taters into big taters."

Guernsey Cows

Doy Caldwell pulled off the road and went down a short, steep drive and then across the creek on a cement crossing—people called that kind of crossing a submarine because it was under the water a lot of the time—and on up into the yard. He parked behind a red Chevy pickup with Texas plates beneath a sprawling sugar maple and sat quiet in his car. Silent for a moment, listening to the sound of water coming up from the creek, but then a sturdy gray-haired lady came bustling around the corner of the house. Mary Isenhart.

"Deputy!" she said cheerily. "I'm so glad you're here!"

Doy got out of his car. "They told me something about keys...."

"Caldwell!" Mrs. Isenhart was peering squinting at his name tag. "You're related to those Caldwells over around Conings?"

"My uncle," Doy said. "My great-uncle, my dad's uncle...." Doy felt oddly flustered. People always wanted to know where you were from, who you were related to. Mrs. Isenhart was just being friendly. But still. All the questions. Doy took a breath, looked her in the face—sunlight coming through the leaves glittering off her glasses. He said, "But I grew up over in Upshur County."

"Well, I'm glad you're here, anyway." Mrs. Isenhart put a hand on his arm.

Yes, her keys were locked in the car. That was her problem. Why she called the law. Locked up in her car, and she couldn't find her spare key. She turned the house over, too. Doy nodded, kept nodding, and he got the slim jim from the trunk of his car and then followed her around the side of the house to the back. Her car, an older but spotless and clean Dodge Colt, was parked by the kitchen door. Mrs. Isenhart didn't know what she'd do if she couldn't get in her car and drive somewhere. What if her husband took sick? He was an old man and might get sick any time. He was 93 years old! He might get sick. It happened. Younger men than him got sick. And even if he didn't get sick, they'd starve to death when the garden played out and she couldn't get to the store. It was just a tragedy waiting to happen. And all because of a key. A key!

Doy listened to her talk about the tragedy and thought she seemed pretty cheerful about it all, though. He listened, and then he ran the strip of metal down inside the door, and opened it. Took maybe thirty seconds. Maybe twenty.

"Well!" Mrs. Isenhart said. "We're saved!"

Doy stepped back a bit. "It's nothing."

"Oh, no, you saved our lives," Mrs. Isenhart said.

"Well...."

"Come on inside," Mrs. Isenhart said. "Have a nice glass of ice tea. Come on."

After a moment, Doy followed Mrs. Isenhart to the house. She kept talking the whole time—glad she could go somewhere in her car, she said, she was a goer. Always going someplace. Go to church on Sunday now. Reverend Snider from Parkersburg was going to preach. She'd seen him before—he always got so excited when he preached. And she could go to Weston, too, she cooked and cleaned a couple of times a week for old Rence Talbot—did Doy know old Rence Talbot? Lawrence Talbot. Brother to that old Kline Talbot in Burnt House. She helped him, too, three times a week. Just a little cooking, a little cleaning. Keeping that sad old man company. A little money didn't hurt—now that she could go driving, why, she'd be doing good for people and making money, too! Always going somewhere, always doing things—

Doy came through the door, Mrs. Isenhart still talking, and into the kitchen. Two men sat at the table, remains of a big dinner spread out before them. Old Mr. Isenhart, 93 years old and he looked every day of it, all wrinkled and shriveled and bald and bent over, though alert and twinkly, too. The other man much younger, in his 30s, maybe, a relative of some sort visiting from Texas, maybe a nephew. He introduced himself but Doy didn't quite catch the name. Seemed friendly enough, though.

"Well, we got us a lawman here," old Mr. Isenhart said, squinting through his wrinkles.

Doy stood smiling, smiling a bit shyly, with the slim jim in his hand, holding it dangling at his side. This sort of thing was hard to do sometimes for Doy, talking to strangers about nothing, going into their houses. But the Isenharts all seemed like nice people.

"You all go out on the front porch," Mrs. Isenhart ordered. "I'll bring you something to drink."

Doy stood aside while the two men got up from the table. The nephew or whatever stood aside, too, and let old Mr. Isenhart lead the way through the house all hunched over and leaning forward on his cane. He scooted right along, though. The walls of the front room were covered with pictures—nieces, nephews, kids, grandkids, brothers, sisters, grandparents—the Isenharts had a lot of relatives. They went on out and sat on the porch, looking down on the big maple, Doy's patrol car, the green lawn sloping down to Cove Creek.

"That was pretty slick," the younger man said. The nephew or whatever. A schoolteacher of some sort, Doy sort of thought Mrs. Isenhart had said. Maybe a school principal. "You got right in that car. I would've had to break a window, I bet."

"Now, I don't want you breaking out the windows on my car." Mrs. Isenhart bustled out carrying a tray with three glasses of tea.

"I didn't say I wanted to—or that I was going to. Only that was the only way I knew—to." He laughed and took a glass.

"Well, I don't care." Mrs. Isenhart disappeared back inside.

"Caldwell." The old man was squinting at Doy's name tag. There came that name thing again. That family thing. The old man asked, "You related to those Caldwells over by Conings?"

"Right—but I was raised over in Upshur County," Doy said again.

"I worked with one of those Caldwells once," the old man said. "On a pipeline crew. I worked for the Eureka"— he called it *you-reeky*—"Pipeline Company, years and years ago. We laid pipe all over this part of the country."

"Uh-huh." Doy sipped his tea.

"Oh, that was hard work. That was real hard work— out there laying pipe in all weathers. Cold. Hot. I'd rather farm, myself." The old man nodded and kept nodding as he talked. "Now, farming's hard work, too, but at least you're your own boss. Yes, sir, I like farming. No money in it though. Hard way to make a living, it's real hard...."

Old Mr. Isenhart talked about as much as his wife. Doy wondered what their evenings were like—did they just chatter away at each other? Or maybe they were all talked out and just sat around silently moping.

"...and then there's all that crime!" The old man was staring at Doy.

"Huh?" Doy asked. "What?"

"That crime—all that crime they're having these days that you have to deal with."

"Oh," Doy said. "No, it's pretty quiet around here most of the time."

Mr. Isenhart looked at Doy, his mouth open a little, scraggly teeth working a little. He was disappointed.

"But," Doy said, "you know, there was a kid over by the college last week got his camera stole out of his car."

"Stole his camera!" Old Mr. Isenhart was astounded. "Right out of his car!"

"Oh, there's some young boys out there causing trouble," Doy said. He nodded. "We try to keep an eye on them."

Mrs. Isenhart bustled out and sat down.

"Mother, there was a camera stole out of a car over in Glenville last week," Mr. Isenhart said. He liked having news to share.

"Oh, it's getting bad out there," Mrs. Isenhart said.

"But it's not violent," the relative from Texas said. "You're all pretty safe here."

"Oh, no, there's shootings here," the old man said. "It's getting bad."

Everyone looked at Doy. He sat up a little in his chair. Looked down at the creek—a kingfisher sitting on a fencepost looking down at the water.

"Oh, I don't know," Doy said. The kingfisher flew away upstream. Doy looked back at everyone on the porch. "There hasn't been anything bad for a few years."

"Well, I think everything's just going to get worse," Mrs. Isenhart said.

Doy shrugged. "I guess it will...."

"You get to see it all," Mr. Isenhart said.

There wasn't too much all of what they wanted to hear about, violent crime. In five or six years, there hadn't been too much of that violence. A fight every now and then, but that didn't count. There was that teenaged boy over in Sand Fork shot his daddy after an argument, and maybe he should have, the old man had been beating on him for years. And there was a man who bought and sold oil leases got shot in the nuts over near Cedarville, but everybody knew about that. Payback of some sort.

"It's just not too violent around here," Doy said.

"It will be, I bet," Mrs. Isenhart said. Such a cheerful lady, and so gloomy. "You watch the news, things are getting bad—and they'll get worse. Old Mr. Talbot, now, he says there'll be a revolution in this country."

"And then the Russians will come in and take over, right," the nephew from Texas said. He was probably joking. He was smiling, at least.

"Well, no—well, there was that Heckert boy shot himself last month!" Mr. Isenhart got excited again. He scooted up on his chair and leaned forward on his cane. "That was real bad! Real bad. I wonder why he did that. I wonder why he shot himself. I heard he just laid himself out under a tree and shot himself."

Doy nodded. "I was the first one out there...."

"You say you were the first one out there!" Mr. Isenhart's eyes were all glittery. Eager. "Well, what happened? Why'd he do that? Why'd he go and kill himself?"

"I guess some people just can't take it anymore," the nephew said.

Doy looked back out down at the yard again. The Heckert boy's body had been stretched out under a massive black locust that stood all alone in the middle of a rolling pasture alongside Leading Creek, a few milling tan-and-white Guernsey cows keeping it company. Mr. and Mrs. Heckert were waiting at the pasture gate looking—blasted, shocked, not crying but just totally at a loss. A neighbor lady had her hand on Mrs. Heckert's shoulder but Mrs. Heckert just stared around witlessly, redeyed, and Mr. Heckert said, "He's out there" and pointed. Doy slowly drove his car out across the meadow over the soft soggy spring grass and came up to the tree. Amazing, that giant tree out there by itself, all these years nobody'd cut it down for fence posts. Think of all the fence posts you could get out of that tree. And there the Heckert boy was, dead, sprawled clumsily out and broken, the top of his head gone. Doy stayed in his car and waited for the ambulance to come from Weston, and he had to wait a long time.

"But why do you think he went and did it?" old Mr. Isenhart asked.

"I don't know," Doy said. If there had been a note or anything, the boy's parents had carried it away.

"Some people just can't take it anymore," the nephew from Texas said again, and he sounded so bitter that everyone broke from their thoughts and looked at him. He looked back. Not smiling, now. He looked back at them all. "Well, they can't!"

Later, after he left the Isenharts, Doy pulled his car over at the top of a hill and looked out down and over at the Heckert farm. They'd buried the boy under the big locust, and now Doy could see Mr. Heckert's truck out there in the field, parked by the grave, and Mr. Heckert hard at work putting up a fence around the grave site to keep the cows from tramping it down. Come summertime those cows were going to miss the shade of that tree, Doy thought. What a waste. He sat watching for a long time, until he finally gave up and drove on back to town.

Part Two
Dropsy and Heart Trouble

Be Patient

Even when I was in college I would go back to Burnt House in the summer, at least for a little while, and stay with Gran in the house up off Horn Creek, and almost every day I'd walk or drive down and spend some time with Pap Talbot, my mom's dad, who lived in that house alone after Grammaw Talbot died. He liked it when I read to him, though he had me doing some other things, too— walk up the road to the post office in the mornings to get the mail, or drive him to a doctor's appointment, and once or twice he had me out there mowing the yard. But mostly it was reading: the *Wall Street Journal* or *Forbes* or the Clarksburg newspaper or the Glenville or Weston newspapers. Sometimes I'd read from whatever book I was dragging along that summer, and he thought *Fear of Flying* was silly and embarrassing, and he thought the hunting scene at the end of *Song of Solomon* was unrealistic ("the woman who wrote that book never went hunting," he said). But he liked to listen to almost anything I read.

This was all after he'd chased off the rest of the family by being horrible and cruel and bullying and mean-spirited and miserly. He lived alone because just about everyone hated him. I knew how he treated people—I knew about his pettiness and his tantrums, about his bitter penny-pinching greed, about his hard cold anger toward the world and almost everyone in it—and almost every bad thing people said about him was true. But he liked me, for some reason. You might not believe how kind and considerate he was to me, mostly. People aren't all one way all the time.

One day I got there a bit early, and he sent me walking up the road to the post office to get the mail, and Bess Wiant, the postmistress, was still working in the back with one of the letter carriers, and she leaned out the service window and said, "I guess you're here to pick up Kline's mail?"

"Yeah, I am," I said.

"Well, we're not ready yet." Bess got back to work. She and the delivery guy would sort the mail back in the room behind the window and stuff it into the mailboxes with rustling papery popping thunking sounds.

"I guess Pap thought the mail was up," I said.

"Well, he should know better," Bess said. She kept on working, thunking the mail into the boxes.

"I can wait," I said. I sat back on a stool next to the service window. I loved that little post office: it smelled like wood and wax, and there was always a big pile of WANTED posters to look through. So I sat and smelled the clean wax smell and looked at pictures of criminals and wondered who they really were and listened to Bess chunk the mail into the boxes. After a few minutes she slowed down, and quit. Then she leaned out the window.

"Your granddad is the most impatient man I ever knew," she said.

I said, "Well...."

"It's true! I've known him almost sixty years!"

"Yeah?" I sat back, waiting for a story. That was always the best part of being home, waiting for a story.

"Kline—well, your grandma, Alma." Bess was still talking out the service window, bent over a table in the back room looking at me. "You remember how hard she worked, right?"

"Sure," I said. "She was always doing something."

"Okay, well, they used to keep chickens—everybody did, then, a long time ago. And Kline, he's greedy as well as he's impatient, and he always wanted more—more chickens, more eggs. Of course, it was Alma had to do most of the work, or the girls when they got big enough. But Kline would do one thing with those chickens by himself, and he didn't trust anyone else to do it. He'd go out there to the hen house with an awl or a nail or a pocketknife and chip away at those eggs, pick the shells off so the baby chicks would be born a day or two early and start growing quicker. He didn't trust nature. He couldn't ever wait for nature."

"Wow!"

"Oh, he'd go out in the garden and flick dirt off the bean sprouts when they were coming up, so they'd all grow faster."

I laughed at that one.

"You laugh, now, but that man can be terrible," Bess said. "He did the same thing when Alma was pregnant with your Aunt Irene. He got her born early."

"No way!"

Bess stepped back from the window and went around and came out into the waiting room.

"It's true," she said. "Alma went into labor, or thought she did, and old Kline got in his truck and drove to Alum Bridge—that's where the paved road from Weston ended in those days, at Alum Bridge, it was just mud between here and there. And Kline got his car out of the garage he kept it in and drove on into Weston on the paved road and he got the doctor." Bess caught her breath, a gasp. "And so then he drove the doctor back to Alum Bridge, and they got in his truck and they drove back through the mud to Burnt House. And when they got here, Alma wasn't in labor anymore."

Bess looked at me and nodded. So there!

After a moment, I asked, "And...."

"And so Kline told that doctor, he said, I'm not bringing you all the way out here a second time. He said, you need to get in there and get me that baby right now. Right *now*. And the doctor did it—brought out that baby two or three days early, a week early, I don't know."

"Wow."

I thought of poor Grammaw Talbot. Back in one of those bedrooms, pregnant, sick and miserable. Alone, I guessed. Full of a baby. And how did that doctor get Irene out? Some drug? Did he cut the baby out of her? Pull it? Did he hook the baby to a chain and winch it out not really ready to live and leave poor Grammaw all ripped apart and bloody? Ah, wow. Disgusting. I almost felt a cramp myself. I never wanted kids. I touched my belly. Sick.

I said, "Jeeze."

"That's right!" Bess said. "And so that's how your Aunt Irene was born. And I've always thought that was why she's always had all those problems she has—she was just born too soon."

Bess brought out the day's mail and handed it to me: Wall Street Journal, Clarksburg Exponent, some bills and bank statements.

"You need to tell that old man he needs to learn how to wait."

"I will," I said.

"Your granddad's too old to hurry. There's only one place he's a-going to."

I walked back to Pap's house along the broken asphalt rim of the road. Summer morning. Still cool. Sun shining. Pap was inside the house sitting by the fire in his wheelchair. I handed him the mail.

"Took a while," he said.

I said, "Bess says you need to learn some patience."

"Hell's fire," Pap said. He looked the mail over. Squinted at the newspapers. Didn't look at me. Finally he said, "Well, maybe I do."

Eternity

Four days a week Mary Isenhart worked for old man Talbot, Kline Talbot, long retired from working for the Eureka Pipeline company, who lived there in Burnt House after his wife, Alma, died. His younger grandson, Mark, was staying with him then, and Mark was taking some time out from college and was sort of lost in the world, a sad boy, and he would drive the old man to the doctor when he had to go, or he'd run errands to town, to the bank, or the store, and he mowed the yard and did various little jobs around the house. But Mary did the important work, cleaning and cooking and laundry, and making sure Talbot was clean and well-fed. Not that it ever helped his temper—Talbot was known in the community for being mean to his family.

Mary worried about the old man and his grandson. Families were supposed to be about love, she thought, but these Talbots were different. Mark had a little girlfriend who lived up Hog Run, but she was young and she didn't count, really, she didn't know anything about the world, and Mark's mother was off near Minneapolis or someplace teaching school, and she didn't want to have anything to do with anything in Burnt House or anyone in it, and so the boy was stuck with Kline Talbot, and Kline Talbot was so mean so much of the time. Cruel. It was sad, she thought. Families weren't supposed to be that way, or any one person so cruel.

Now it was in October, late October, and it was getting chilly and rainy out, and the leaves were mostly down, and the old man decided it was time to visit the grave of his first wife, who had died years and years before. He did that once or twice a year, he'd go out there to that cemetery, a Catholic cemetery back on top of a hill, and place flowers on the grave.

It was something Talbot would put a lot of planning into: for a week or more he would pay close attention to the TV weatherman, and he would totter outside and stand on the porch and study the clouds, and then the night before he would bathe and shave carefully, or as best he could, and then set out his one black suit, ancient clothes that sagged and bagged on him—he'd gotten skinny as he aged. When she was alive, Alma, his second wife, would watch him prepare, year after year, but she never said anything about it or asked anything about it. Talbot was a private man, and that other woman's death so long ago was private, and it was his business. One day Talbot took a box of his first wife's letters and photos from the cellar and carried it out behind the barn and burned the box and everything in it. Alma later found a few photos and letters that he had missed, and she showed them to Mary—that first wife had been young and pretty and a Catholic. But just about everything else about her was always a mystery.

Talbot drove himself to the grave as long as he could drive, and when he got too old he would get a grandson to drive him, if one was available and he wasn't too otherwise mad at them, so now it was late October and time to go to the grave, and Mark was there, and it was Mark's job to drive. That was the plan, at least. Mary Isenhart came around to work that day and found the old man sitting in the dining room in his wheelchair sipping from a saucer of coffee.

"Good morning, there!" Mary said. She was always naturally cheerful, but she made a point to be especially cheerful around old Kline. She thought it was maybe good for him, maybe it would rub off, maybe if he saw other people being cheerful he could be cheerful, too.

Talbot turned slowly and looked over his shoulder at her with his unblinking pale hard gray blue eyes. He said, "Morning."

Well, Mary thought. He's more quiet than usual. Maybe more mad, too, about something. Oh, well. It probably was going to be a long day.

"You got your coffee, I see," Mary said. She bustled by him to the kitchen. "You want some bacon? Some nice oatmeal?"

"Anything's fine," Talbot said. "I don't care."

There was a lot of laundry to do, and some mopping, but Mary really wanted to go to the cemetery with Kline and Mark. She was curious—she liked knowing things about people, and that dead first wife was a mystery. Also, she'd never been to a Catholic cemetery and that was something, too.

After the old man finished eating, Mary roused Mark up from his bedroom in the basement—Mark was depressed and sullen and spent so much time down there—and he came up and backed the old black Rambler out of the garage and parked it up in front of the house. The house was built on the lower side of the hill from the road, and Talbot, somber in his black suit, pulled himself up the steps with one hand on the railing and one hand on his cane.

"Need a hand, old-timer?" Mary asked.

"I'll make it, by God," the old man said.

Mark stayed in the car, didn't get out to open the door for his granddad or do anything to help him. Just sat there behind the wheel looking grumpy and unhappy. Mary went quickly up the back steps and came around and opened the door for Talbot.

"Now you just get in, Kline, and we'll be all set," Mary said. "Mark, you want to check and make sure he's settled in there safe?"

Mark asked, "What?"

Talbot lowered himself into the front seat—heavily, for such a skinny old man—with a grunt, and Mary went back down the steps and made sure the house was locked up safe and then came around and stood next to the car door. Mark was sitting behind the wheel staring straight ahead, looking at nothing.

"Now, Mark, you're going to have to move so I can get in, or else I'll have to crawl over top of you."

It was a two-door car. Mary stood there smiling at the boy.

"What?" Mark looked up at her. "Oh—sorry." He got out of the car and folded the seat up for Mary.

Mary patted him on the shoulder. "You're a good boy—you were just thinking."

Talbot said, "Shit." He was staring straight ahead, too. These men like to stare.

"Well, here we are," Mary said. "All ready to go off on a nice trip."

"Some trip," Mark said. Sulky.

Gravel crunched under the tires and the car pulled onto the road and around a slight curve. In front of Butchie's store, Claudie was standing in the doorway looking out and she peered at the car through her glasses. Mary waved.

"That Claudie's a woman who eats well," Talbot said.

"Well, she always was stout," Mary said. "Her mother, too. It's in the family, I expect."

"I'd hate to be the one a-buying her food," Talbot said. "She'll probably put that store out of business."

They drove on out of the town and toward Troy, and Linn, and on toward Weston. It was a drizzly, gray day with low misty clouds, and leaves were coming off the trees, and Mary pointed out at the houses they passed that had nice, clean yards, and the houses where the leaves were all piled up and wet and sloppy-looking. Talbot didn't say much. Mark just drove. When they came through Weston, they passed the turnoff to go down to Rence Talbot's house—Kline's older brother—and when Mary said they might stop by and say hello, Talbot shook his head again.

"He's just watching his TV, or sleeping," Talbot said.

"We could maybe take him with us," Mary said.

"He don't want to go with us," Talbot said.

"Well, it's right on the way," Mary said. "I thought we might cheer the old feller up."

"He don't need cheering up."

Mary thought, poor old Rence likes a joke as much as Kline likes a scowl and he's sitting there in that little house all alone and lonely. Rence sure needed cheering up. All these people need cheering up. This whole family needed cheering up. But she didn't say anything. They went on through Weston and down a county road paralleling the interstate, then pulled away and headed up into the hills—the last road up to the old Catholic cemetery. Mary thought of the preacher Sunday at her own church.

"You know, we had us a preacher come in from Ohio," Mary said. "And he was a fat little feller, and he was so excited about the Word that he was almost dancing up there in front."

"Huh." Talbot just looked out the window at the trees. He didn't care much for church, or hearing about church.

"And he was about half-bald, and he was all combed-over, and when he got excited his hair was all flying out and standing up, and some people were laughing at him a little, and he knew it, and he laughed too and shook his head, and his hair was flying around, and he said, 'Judge not, lest ye be judged!'"

"He make that line up himself?" Mark asked. He hadn't said much more than two words all the way from

Burnt House. Not pouty. But not happy at all, either. He hadn't wanted to come, but he didn't argue about it any. Still a boy, not thinking like a man.

"Oh, it was just the funniest thing," Mary said. "It was the way he said it, you know. He really meant it! And I was driving over to the house this morning, and I went past where that Lyman Whiting lives—"

"Lyman Whiting," Talbot repeated. He hadn't said much, either, but at least he was listening. "He was married to that Altop woman before she died."

"That's right—"

"That Nelly Altop."

"That's right—"

"I knew him. He used to work driving a truck for Dowell when they first came into this country. Then his woman died."

"That's right," Mary said quickly, and caught her breath. "And so now he's living all squalid-like and poor, cars broke down in his yard, and his house needs painting, and I drove by and I saw him out there—and then I heard a voice say, 'Judge not, lest ye be judged.'"

"God talked to you?" Mark asked.

"Oh, He talks to me all the time," Mary said. She laughed. "Yeah! Just this morning he talked to me again, He said, 'Blessed are the peacemakers.'"

"Peacemakers got a lot of work cut out for them around here," Mark said.

"That why I'm so blessed!" Mary laughed again. "I'm always busy looking after you two!"

Mark shook his head and Mary reached up and patted him on the shoulder. These two did need a peacemaker a lot of the time, the boy sullen and sad, and the old man bitter and cruel, neither one speaking to the other for days at a time except through her. It had to be a lonely way to live.

The car came up out of the trees then into a clearing with a big white cross outlined against the low gray sky.

Then Mary saw the chapel, neat and white and well-maintained, and the graves stretching off across the hilltop. But first there was that big cross rising out of the stone base.

"That's where they buried that monsignor, that preacher they used to have," Talbot said. "They sure all thought they loved that man."

Poor old Talbot sounded like he thought they were a bunch of liars, or fools.

Mark pulled around to the front of the church and parked. The hard rain of the morning had stopped but the clouds were all close and damp, mist blowing through the trees. Foggy. Mark got out of the car so Mary could get out and go around and help Talbot, and the old man emerged slowly from the car, Mary holding his arm, and he stood unsteadily on the gravel, peering around.

"Well, we made it!" Mary tried to be cheerful.

In her married family, the Isenharts—but growing up, too, in the Waughs—they'd all get together in the springtime and go out on a weekend—Decoration Day, Memorial Day—and clean and clear the old family cemeteries and visit and picnic, and it wasn't sad at all—well, not too sad, sometimes people would tear up some, cry a little, thinking about all the people who'd been loved and had gone on—not really sad, though, it was a time to be with family, and have fun, and love each other. But these Talbots, they weren't much for fun or love or even being around people, not even each other. Mary decided again to act cheerful, anyway—to act normal, even if she had to force it. She said, "We've sure had a good trip so far!"

Mark shook his head and wandered away down the side of the hill to the outhouse. Mary watched him tug a time or two at the door—locked, probably—and then go on down into the woods.

"That goddamn boy's going to fall down a goddamn well," Talbot said.

"Oh, I expect he'll be fine," Mary said.

"Or else he'll get lost in the woods."

"We'll hear him if he shouts for help."

"He's so stupid he might not know to shout." Talbot looked glumly around, seeing nothing. He said, "My things are in the trunk."

Things. The plastic flowers he'd had her buy. Plastic flowers—real flowers cost money, and plastic lasted longer anyway. They were in the trunk, and Mark had the key.

"Goddamn boy," Talbot said.

Mary saw Mark come out of the woods down at the far end of the cemetery. "I'll go get him," she said.

Mark was wandering around looking at tombstones when Mary caught up with him. He brightened when he saw her coming up, young-looking again.

"Some of these graves are really old," Mark said. "There's people here born in 1815, 1810, 1820...."

"I guess this is an old part of the country," Mary said.

"They're almost all from Ireland. Pap told me once they were all brought over to work on the railroads."

"Well, some of them lived a long time, too." Mary was bent over, looking at the dates on the stones.

"Look what I found." Mark led her over to the edge of the cemetery, where the graves sloped down to the woods. There was a groundhog hole there—and, down the hill a bit, scattered in the muddy red dirt, two or three big bones. Pieces of an arm, maybe.

"I'd put those back in the hole, except the groundhog'll just toss 'em out again." Mark touched a bone with the toe of his boot. "Nobody's going to need these, anyway."

"You don't know that," Mary said. "Something might. Somebody might." She was aware without turning around that old Talbot was looking their way, watching, waiting, impatient. He didn't like to wait. Sometimes he was just too much.

But—judge not! Judge not.

Mary found a stick and pushed the bones up the slope

and sort of nudged them into the hole. When she looked up, Mark was smiling at her.

"Good work."

"Somebody might need that arm," Mary said. Didn't Catholics believe in full-body resurrection? She'd heard that somewhere. Wasn't that why they had to be buried off by themselves in their own churchyards? Something like that. So Jesus would know where to look. She didn't know any Catholics but that sounded true enough. Mary kicked some muddy clods of earth into the hole. Mark was probably right, of course—the old groundhog would probably push it all out again. But still.

"Come on." Mary touched Mark's arm. "Your granddad needs the car keys."

"Oh." Mark dug around in his pocket and brought out the car keys and offered them to Mary.

"No," Mary said. "He needs you, too. Now, come on."

They walked toward Talbot through the graves, Talbot still standing watching them in his somber baggy black suit next to the black car, dark misty trees closing in all around the hilltop.

"I remember my old granddad," Mary said. "We'd go drive to town or someplace, and we'd go past a cemetery, and he'd always ask, 'I wonder how many dead people are in that graveyard?' And we were a bunch of kids, then, you know, we didn't know anything, and he'd laugh and he'd say 'All of 'em are dead!'"

Mark said, "Yeah?"

"And we'd just laugh, too, like that was the funniest thing," Mary said. "We'd laugh and laugh."

"I bet."

"We were just kids, though. We didn't know anything."

Talbot was still staring at them with his flat cold pale gray eyes when they got up to the car. He said, "The trunk's locked."

"Oh," Mark said.

He opened the trunk and stood out of the way. Inside

the trunk Talbot kept enough tools for almost any situation that involved fixing a car or getting it out of a ditch—wrenches, hammers, jack stands and a handyman jack, two spare tires, and a pair of overalls to wear over his going-to-town clothes so he wouldn't get dirty crawling around in the mud. Also, now, a brown paper bag with the plastic flowers—a half-dozen tulips, red and yellow. Mary took the bag and shut the trunk.

"Now, then," Mary said. "Where do we take these?"

Talbot led the way—slowly—over to the edge of the cemetery, where the open ground began to slope down into the woods. The mist was closing in, fog, Mary noticed, and the old man's jacket was getting damp. He was walking as straight as he could, though. Poor old man. He went a little way along the top of the hill, and then stopped next to a fine big sugar maple. Mary came up next to him and they were standing almost at the foot of a grave, and the grave's tombstone, a big solid-looking piece of black marble read TALBOT carved across the top and MARGARET MARY O'CONNOR TALBOT 1899-1918 across the bottom. There were two O'Connor stones nearby— Margaret's parents, Mary figured from the dates, and maybe the family of a brother. We all come to it someday, Mary thought. Ready or not. Catholic or not. Here we are, Jesus. Come find us. She pulled the flowers from the bag and placed them against the stone. They stood there looking at the grave, and Mary made a silent prayer— Father, find this Catholic lady and look after her....

There was a low bench beneath the maple, and Talbot took a couple of unsteady steps and sat heavily— no thought for the damp concrete messing up his black clothes. Mary sat next to him and patted him on the knee. She could see Mark wandering down at the far end of the cemetery again looking at old graves.

"It's not that boy's fault," Talbot said. "Well, not all of it. He can't help who he is."

"Well, I know," Mary said.

"If things had gone the way they were supposed to go, he'd never been born."

"It's not his fault," Mary said.

Talbot shook his head. "He should've never been born."

"I know it's been a long time for you," Mary said. She was looking back at the grave. "But it's still sad."

"Well," Talbot said. "When we got over there to France the war was just over, so they just turned around and sent us home. And then when I got off the boat I found out she'd been dead and buried almost a month and nobody got word to me. All I could do then was buy her that stone."

Mary tried to squeeze his hand but he pulled away. She thought, Father, look out for these people....

"It was that Spanish flu," Talbot said. "Killed a lot of people that year, young people—killed all the pregnant women. That's why there's no family buried with her."

They sat under the dripping tree. A red pickup truck came around the bend and headed down the hill.

Talbot said, "It don't mean nothing now."

Baby Never Grew

Vesta Talbot was my grandfather's older sister. I knew
her when I was little—knew her, loved her, my favorite
aunt, a nice old lady who always dressed in green, who
made a skimpy living giving piano lessons at her big
gloomy house in Weston, a lady who made me fudge, who
read me stories and talked about books. Vesta wasn't all
sweet, of course—she was a real person. She could be
bad. I remember them talking about how she killed her
neighbor's tree, a sycamore that dropped leaves in the
yard of her gloomy house, and the leaves made her mad,
so she went out one night and poured vinegar and salt
water all around the roots of the tree and killed it. So I
knew Vesta was ornery. But still—she made me fudge!
She read me stories! She always talked to me when no
one else would. She took me seriously.

When she died suddenly of a stroke I cried and
cried. But even though I was just a kid—a sad kid, at my
first funeral—I noticed through my tears that no one
else was crying. Nobody else even seemed sad. Pap and
Uncle Rence, her brothers, sat stony-faced and grim in
their good black clothes, and my mom sat in the back
with some ladies, talking and laughing about something.
Irene, my mom's sister, my aunt, didn't even come in for

the funeral. There were only six or seven people at the funeral home—only six or seven people, and she'd lived in Lewis County all her life, eighty years or more—and not one of those six or seven was crying except me, and I cried and I cried until Grammaw Talbot grabbed me by the arm and jerked me outside and sat me down hard in the car and told me to be quiet. To stop acting up! To stop embarrassing everyone! Then she went back inside and I sat blubbering in the hot car by myself.

Years later, one summer when I was in high school I was out with Pap Talbot on the porch and Pap was talking about growing up over on Rocky Fork. The people who lived there then were all dead now, I never knew them, they were nothing but names to me, but of course I always liked hearing him talk. I was in the swing reading *Catch-22*, which I didn't like too much then. Didn't dislike it enough to stop reading, but it wasn't as funny as the blurbs on the cover said it was supposed to be. I didn't get it. I kept on reading with mounting irritation I didn't understand. Old Pap kept talking about dead people—Ramseys, Sleeths, Frosts. Hennens. Renners. Fishers. All just names. He was talking to himself more than he was talking to me. Remembering. Then he said something about Aunt Vesta. How Vesta sure thought she loved that Fisher boy. How then she went and poisoned his dog.

Poisoned his dog.

I thought, What?

"Huh?" I asked.

"What?" Pap asked back.

"Somebody poisoned a dog? Vesta poisoned a dog?"

"Oh," Pap said. He leaned forward and tapped out his pipe. "Goddamn Vesta thought she loved that Fisher boy—that Matt Fisher. He was one of those Fishers that lived up above Sand Fork. But he wouldn't have her, so she poisoned his dog."

I leaned up on my elbow and looked disbelievingly at the old man. "What?"

"Your Aunt Vesta, she always thought she was better than everybody else," Pap said. "You know that. She was always acting so big. She was always talking about how she went to college and studied music, how she played the piano, how she wanted to go off to New York and be in an orchestra. Well, shit—me and Rence went to college, too, and you never saw us acting big like that."

"But about the dog." Killing a tree was one sad thing—but killing a dog.

"I guess there's some things you don't need to know." Pap filled his pipe and lit it, put the red Prince Albert can back in his shirt pocket. Puffed a couple of times. I just lay there in the swing, twisted around, watching him. I didn't need to know but I knew he was going to tell me anyway. "Vesta thought she loved that Matt Fisher, but he turned her down, so she poisoned his dog." Puffed. Always a wet sticky sound when he puffed that pipe, I'd been hearing it all my life. "This was after she had that baby that wouldn't grow."

"A baby." I stared at him but he didn't say anything. A baby that wouldn't grow. Vesta's baby. I asked, "Vesta had a baby? That Matt Fisher's baby?"

"I guess," Pap said. "She never would say who the father was."

"She wasn't married."

He said, "No."

I thought for a minute. Tried to do some math in my head. This would have been—the 1910s? The teens, probably. Maybe the 1920s. Not later than that. Maybe earlier. Unmarried and pregnant would have been a big deal, then, in those days, a very big deal. Shameful. Shame for the whole family.

I asked, "So, what happened to the baby?"

Pap shook his head. "Well, that baby wouldn't grow."

"What do you mean?"

"It wouldn't grow...."

"What?"

"That's all."

"It died?"

"Well, later," Pap said. "But the little son of a bitch never would grow. It just lay there in that crib and it wouldn't grow."

That didn't make any sense. The old man made it sound like the baby didn't *want* to grow.

Like it was a bad baby.

I asked, "Why didn't it grow?"

"Hell, I don't know," Pap said. "It just didn't."

"Didn't they take it to the doctor?"

Pap laughed. "Nobody went to the doctor in those days."

"Didn't they feed it?"

"Of course they fed it!" he said. "Jesus Christ!"

There was a glint there. Pap was getting pissed at me. About what? He was the one who brought poor Vesta's dead baby up.

I asked, "But why didn't it grow?"

"I don't know, goddamn it," the old man said. "I told you—it just didn't grow and it later died."

"But—" I said. I was—I don't know—shocked. I had this mental picture of a tiny monster bad baby. "But—that's terrible."

"Now, why the hell are you a-wanting to know about that dead baby?" Pap asked. Now he was really mad.

"I don't know!" I said. I was really mad, too. "Why'd you start talking about it?"

Pap didn't say anything. He just sat there puffing at his pipe.

I opened the book and stared at the pages.

The words made no sense.

Let the Winter In

"It's too damn cold in here," Kline Talbot said.

He shoved aside the grill in front of the fire and turned up the gas. Blue flames turned yellow and orange at the edges and crawled up the clay plates at the back of the stove, and the clay started to glow and cast off more heat. Talbot held his hands out in front of the fire and rubbed them.

"I don't know, Pap, it's already getting pretty hot in here, right?"

Talbot swung around in his chair and watched that damn stupid boy—his grandson, Mark—come into the room carrying a cup of coffee. Mark sat back in the recliner and put his feet up and blew on the cup.

Talbot wondered why anyone would have a hot drink if they don't want it hot.

Blowing on a drink.

That goddamn boy was a goddamn fool.

Mark said, "If you're not careful, we're going to suffocate."

"I pay the goddamn gas bills around this house." Talbot swung back and adjusted the stove's screen, and rolled his chair an inch or two closer to the fire. "By god, I can have it as hot as I damn well want it."

"Well," Mark said, "you know, not everybody likes it hot like this."

"You don't have to stand it if you don't want to," Talbot said. He folded his hands on his lap and stared catlike at the fire. "You can go somewhere else."

Be good if you did go somewhere else, Talbot thought. Be best.

Mark sat and slurped at his coffee noisily. Talbot didn't want to look at him—hell, just hearing that boy was enough. The stove hissed, and now and then a car would go by outside, and he could hear the tires hissing, too, on the cold, wet pavement. Lawrence, Rence, Talbot's brother, was supposed to drive out from Weston, but it snowed in the night, and even though the snow had mostly melted by midmorning the roads were still wet and the air was cold.

"Rence won't come," Talbot said.

Mark said, "I know he shouldn't be driving in this weather."

"Hell, he shouldn't be driving at all—he's in worse shape than I am." Talbot pushed his glasses up his long nose and looked out the window. There were a few snowy spots on the hillside but dead brown leaves and patches of mud were showing through. "And my driving days are long over. Long over."

Mary Isenhart came in from the kitchen, then, wiping her hands on a dishrag.

"You fellers all ready for a good family dinner?" Mary asked.

Talbot didn't want to look at her, either. Always she was too damn cheerful—grinning, smiling. Good morning she'd say when she came in the door. And what the hell was ever good about any goddamn morning? All good mornings were in the past. If there ever were any. And no good mornings to come, either. Good family dinner she said just now. Even if it tasted good—and Mary was a good cook, she was—what the hell would be good about it?

"Rence ain't coming out," Talbot said. "Roads are too damn bad."

"Oh, no, Kline, the roads are fine out today. All the snow's melted away." Mary leaned against the doorframe and looked out the window at the road. A pale blue pickup went by, slowly. "Of course, I wouldn't want to go riding around too much with Rence, myself. I don't think he sees too well, now."

Talbot said, "He's too damn old."

"Well, we'll eat as soon as he gets here." Mary went back to the kitchen.

Talbot turned his chair and wheeled over to the door and looked out the window. Road. Leaves. Water dripping. Hell with it. He spun backwards and took his place by the fire. Looked up at the mantle, and the damn clock was stopped. Talbot stood, slowly, grabbing hold of the mantle.

Mark said from his chair, "You want me to get that?"

"Hell, no." Talbot felt around on the mantle for the key, found it, and began winding the clock. That boy wouldn't know how to wind a clock if you showed him. Fat stupid son of a bitch. Five turns, seven turns, heat from the fire rising good and strong, nine turns and the spring was tight and Talbot set the pendulum to swinging, and he sat back in his chair. He said, "Shit."

"Have it your way," Mark said.

"Don't need your help for nothing."

The clock ticked and the fired hissed. Now and then a car would pass by the house, and Talbot would look up. Finally, he looked up and saw a white car slowly pull up in front of the house, and he heard the sounds of tires crunching on gravel.

"He made it after all," Talbot said. "Hell's fire."

Mark got up from the chair and looked out the window. He said, "It's Rence, all right."

"He's got no business driving out here in weather like this," Talbot said. He looked back at the fire. Even in his driving days he never liked driving in the winter—the damn weather was too damn chancy. Before any trip in the winter he'd stand on the porch and study the sky, trying to figure out what was going to happen. His wife always said he worried too much and the damn kids—when they were little and living in Burnt House and now, too—they couldn't understand just what it was he was doing out on the porch staring at the sky, but if they came out to stand with him he'd just tell them to get the hell back inside, damn little fools.

Mark went out on the porch—and left the door open behind him. Damn boy. Did that on purpose, you know he did. Let the winter in. Talbot scooted over in his chair and shut the door and looked out the window, watched the boy go up the steps and help Rence out of his car. Rence's white Rambler was parked just in front of Talbot's own black one, and Talbot watched the white car's door slowly open and Rence stick his head out and slowly pull himself up out of the car. Rence had a cigar in his mouth and wore a tan jacket. Mark took Rence's elbow and steadied him. It looked like Mark said something, and then Rence said something back, and Mark shut the car door and they came around the car and down the steps and into the house.

"What the hell did you drive all the way out here for?" Talbot asked. He backed his wheelchair up a bit so they could get in the door. "By god, I wouldn't drive in weather like this."

"Oh, the road's pretty good today," Rence said around his cigar. He took off his hat but had trouble holding onto the hat and his cane and unzipping his jacket at the same time. After a moment Mark reached around him and unzipped the jacket and helped him pull it off his shoulders. "I didn't have any trouble getting in."

"Hell you say."

"Want some coffee?" Mark asked. "Pap, you want anything?"

"I don't need nothing."

Mark shrugged and headed off to the kitchen.

"I've got a goddamn doctor appointment tomorrow," Talbot said. "You know those damn doctors don't know nothing."

"Well, it's good to get checked out every now and then," Rence said. He settled down into the couch next to the door.

"Goddamn, once they start doctoring on you, they never want to stop." Talbot wheeled backwards across the room. He got out of the wheelchair and took a few shuffling steps over to his favorite chair by the television. He looked back at Rence. "What about you?"

"Oh, I guess I got dropsy and heart trouble." Rence always said that, Dropsy and heart trouble. A joke, a damn joke. He was as bad as Mary was with her cheery Good Mornings. He always liked laughing when there wasn't anything in life to laugh about. When he was young all he cared about was fun. But there wasn't anything fun about the world, not a thing. Damn fool. Rence took a puff on his cigar. "Yeah, I feel like dropping down, and I just don't have the heart to get up."

"Hell you say," Talbot said. Rence was a damn fool all his life. Making jokes.

Mark came back in with the coffee and set it on the arm of the sofa next to Rence.

"It's too damn dark in here," Talbot said. "Turn on that light for Rence."

Mark reached over and flipped the switch for the overhead light.

"Not that light," Talbot said. The damn boy stood there staring—Talbot pointed, waved his arm. "That light! Turn that damn light on!"

Mark looked confused. He flipped the overhead light off. Stood there gaping.

"No, no!" Talbot glared. Pointed.

The damn boy just stood there, didn't do anything.

"Oh, goddamn you, you fat idiot. Turn that damn light on!"

"Oh, I don't need a light to drink coffee," Rence said. "I can still find the cup."

Mark reached for the lamp by the sofa and turned the switch. "This one?"

"Goddamn you, why didn't you do that the first time?"

"What?" Mark stood looking—something. Standing with his mouth hanging open stupidly. Looking stupid. He finally said, "I didn't know which one you wanted."

"The hell you didn't." Talbot put one big foot up on the wheelchair, using it for a footstool. The boy kept standing there with his mouth open, he looked like he was about to start blubbering. "You goddamn fat idiot."

Rence put his cigar in an ashtray and sipped at his coffee. "Thank you, Mark."

"That boy's so damn fat I think he lost his mind," Talbot said. "Just like his mother, too. She's so fat I don't know how her man can feed her. By god, she comes down here and eats big meals, though, just like that boy. And then he brings that damn girl down here and she eats, too! And I have to pay for it all! I pay for every goddamn thing! Hell, I can't afford to be feeding half the country—I need that money!"

Mark just stood there all shocked and surprised, looking like the goddamn fat idiot he was. Talbot glared at him.

Mary came into the room. "Why, there's old Rence!" She went over, grinning, and patted him on the shoulder. "Hey, old-timer! I knew you'd make it out just fine!"

"This damn boy don't even know which goddamn light to turn on," Talbot said. "He thinks he's so smart."

"Well, I always said one light's as good as another." Mary glanced at Mark and then backed out of the room.

"Goddamn it, Rence, you're lucky you don't have kids—or grandkids. Sons of bitches don't give a damn about anything, they eat up all your food, take all your money. This boy here, he's crazy. He's got no sense at all. Spends every dime he's got. Then he don't even know which light to turn on."

Rence sat his coffee down. Mark still just stood there.

"And then he's got this girl he brings down here—he does it to her right out there on the porch! He does it to her right down there in his room!" Talbot was getting pale, white and pale with red blotches, and his eyes were icy cold. Pointing at the porch, pointing at the door to the basement. Glaring. "Hell, I don't know where they do it all, but I know they do it every chance they get. They're so proud, they think they invented fucking."

Talbot turned and stared at Mark. "She's just using you for free food, you damn dumb son of a bitch, she's just eating up everything I buy and I need that money."

Rence planted his cane on the floor in front of the sofa and pushed himself up. He staggered for a moment, off balance, and then slowly made his way over to the coat rack.

"Where the hell are you going?"

"I think I better leave," Rence said. He struggled with his jacket. Talbot stared at him, not believing he was really leaving.

"Hell's fire," Talbot said. "You just got here."

"I better leave," Rence said again. He put on his hat and went out. Mark followed him.

"Sure, go out there and talk about me, goddamn you."

Mark shut the door and Talbot could see the top of his head as he stood on the porch. Talbot got up and into his chair and he scooted over to the door and then he could see Mark standing there better, see Rence slowly climb the steps up to the berm and walk around the front of his car and get in. Try to get in. He had a hard time opening the door. Mark just stood there, stupid boy.

Mary came in out of the kitchen. "Is Rence leaving?"

"Hell, I don't know." Talbot was watching out the window.

Outside a log truck came by and had to pull into the far lane to avoid hitting Rence, still trying to fold himself into the car. He finally got in, though. Mark still stood there dumbly.

Mary said, "Well, I'm just surprised he's leaving all of a sudden like that."

Finally, Rence's white car drove slowly away, and Mark turned to come back inside. Talbot scooted his chair back in front of the fire.

Mark came in and shut the door. He said, "Pap, you were wrong there."

Talbot sat back. That goddamn boy. "For what?"

"For how you acted just there—for how you drove Uncle Rence off."

"Who the hell are you to judge me?" Talbot looked from Mark to Mary and back to Mark. "If you'd knowed what light to turn on, he might have stayed."

Mary quietly backed out of the room. Mark stood with tears in his eyes. Twenty-one years old and tearing up like a little girl.

"I didn't know what you wanted," Mark said. "Nobody knows what you want."

"Shit," Talbot said. "I just want to be treated decent."

"What?"

Asking what.

Standing there asking what.

Who ever heard of such a thing—near-grown man standing crying there asking what.

"You son of a bitch," Talbot said. He rolled his chair forward a few inches, leaned forward, too. "You damn dumb son of a bitch, you sit here in this room and argue with me about what's on the damn TV. You want to watch cartoons! You argue with me about what's in the damn newspaper. You argue with me about baseball! You just dispute me over every god damned thing!"

"I do not!"

"You're disputing me right now!"

Mark just stood there. He said, "Well, no...."

"And you're lazy, too," Talbot said. "Grown man and you don't do nothing all day. By God, when I was six years old I was out working in the fields. All day! Hell's fire, I started working in the fields before I started going to school—and before I was old enough to work, I was out there a-carrying water to the men who were a-working."

"I know that," Mark said.

"You're just lazy is all. You're good for nothing, you'd been better off not being born—and you know that, goddamn you."

Talbot looked at Mark standing there.

Talbot said, "You're nothing but a wasted fuck."

The clock ticked, the fire hissed. Outside a car went down the road.

Mark said, "Maybe you should start looking for a new grandson."

Talbot asked, "What?"

But Mark was already on his way down the stairs to the basement, to his bedroom, his little hidy-hole. Talbot wheeled around and sat facing the fire, glaring at the glowing red clay. That boy didn't know a goddamn thing about nothing—and that girl, too. Watch TV, fuck, eat all the food. That's all they did. Sleep. Lazy. Goddamn.

Mary stuck her head in from the dining room and looked around. "Where's Mark?" she asked. "Dinner's about ready."

"Don't worry," Talbot said. "That damn boy won't miss a meal."

"Well, you come on, then, Kline."

"All right." Talbot slowly turned the chair and rolled along after Mary into the dining room. There was a big plate of fried chicken in the center of the table, along with pickled beans, mashed potatoes, gravy, biscuits, and beets.

"Got enough food here for a week," Talbot said.

"You get started," Mary said. "I'll go check on Mark."

"That damn boy," Talbot said. He was already eating. That boy never could do anything right. Tried to show him—tried to teach him. Thought he knew everything already. Dumb son of a bitch was raised wrong. He was just a wasted fuck. His parents should have taken the night off that night—watch TV, play cards, do anything but make Mark. He was sure a wasted fuck.

"Well...." Mary came back in and sat down at the far end of the table. "Now, Mark says he's not feeling like coming up for dinner."

Talbot grunted.

"He says he doesn't want to drive you up to Morgantown tomorrow."

"Damn boy," Talbot said.

"I'm not very hungry," Mary said. She put a drumstick on her plate, and a little dab of mashed potatoes.

"We don't need him," Talbot said. "I don't need him."

"Well," Mary said. "Well, you know I'm working for Mrs. Radcliffe tomorrow—she's been sick-like and has all that laundry to do. So I won't be able to take you to the doctor like you want."

"Hell's fire." Talbot kept on eating.

"Otherwise I would."

"I know that," Talbot said. He poked at a piece of chicken. "Maybe I can still drive."

"Oh, Kline," Mary said. "You know you can't drive all that way."

Talbot didn't say anything.

Mary asked, "You want me to cancel that appointment for you?"

"Don't bother."

"You'll call them?" Mary looked at Talbot. He didn't like using the phone.

"Maybe that boy'll change his mind," Talbot said. "Maybe somebody else can give me a ride."

"I don't think he's going to change his mind," Mary said. "I'll ask around, but it's pretty short notice. You sure you don't want me to cancel for you? Maybe I can drive you up there next week sometime."

"Damn doctors. They don't know nothing." Talbot swallowed heavily and looked straight ahead at the wall and shook his head. "Damn boy."

Hours later, toward evening, and the boy was still hiding down in his bedroom. Sleeping, hiding—same thing. Hiding.

He thought, I'll show that son of a bitch. Prove I can drive a damn car.

Talbot slowly got dressed. Slow—that was it. Nothing wanted to go on right. Shoes. Then a sweater—it was cold out there. Old red and black-checkered wool hunting jacket. Old leather hat with earflaps. Putting it all on took a while. Talbot kept expecting that boy to come upstairs, at least come up and go to the kitchen to get something to eat. He didn't miss many meals, ever. But the damn boy stayed hid.

Shit.

If that boy's too proud to drive, Talbot thought, I'll just go ahead and drive myself.

See if I can't!

It was 100 miles to the hospital in Morgantown, just over 100 miles. Twenty-five miles to Weston, and then another 75 or so on I-79 to the clinic at the university. He'd made the trip often enough, he could probably drive it himself, even on the four-lane.

Dressed finally.

Talbot took the car keys from the mantel and went to the door and out to check on the car. It was cold and damp out on the porch, cold from the patches of snow even though the snow was almost gone, and water was running off the hills. Talbot made his way up the steps, holding onto his cane with one hand and the railing with the other, and then down the berm to the car. The door was unlocked. Tossed the cane in, slid onto the seat. Key fit, and he started to turn it and start the car, but something was wrong. Gas pedal—his foot kept sliding off the gas pedal and flopping around. Something was wrong down there. Couldn't see what it was, though.

Talbot opened the door and stumbled back out of the car and into the road. An oncoming pickup truck had to swerve around him. But Talbot caught his balance and bent back into the car and looked down at the shadowy muddy floor.

He said, "Son of a bitch."

The gas pedal was missing. Gone. Gone! Talbot bent over as best he could and felt around down there but there was nothing. The pedal was gone.

"That goddamn son-of-a-bitch."

The pedal was gone. Nothing left but a piece of metal sticking up from the floor. That goddamn boy did it—Talbot knew it, he knew it—that son of a bitch took the pedal off so nobody could drive the car but him.

Sabotage!

He thought he was so goddamn smart.

Well, to hell with him.

Talbot lowered himself back onto the seat. Felt around on the floor with his feet—heavy shoes made it hard, too, dammit—for the metal sticking up, for the pedal's shaft. The lever. Goddamn it to hell. Found it though. Turned the key, pressed down on the shaft—and the old car started right up. Well!

Pressed then on the brake, pulled the transmission down into drive, switched his foot back to the pedal wire, and the car moved.

Driving, damn it.

Then his foot slipped off and the car stalled out. Went about six feet total.

Goddamn goddamn.

Started the damn car up again. Pressed on the shaft—carefully, concentrating on keeping his big flat foot on that goddamn metal tit son of a bitch, and the car moved. Drove.

Slowly.

Went down through town.

Like almost always, fat Claudie Butcher was out sweeping at the mud in front of the store, and she stopped her goddamn sweeping to watch. Always a big fat woman. Talbot looked at her and nodded—tried to nod—but his foot slipped off the goddamn post and the car suddenly slowed. He got his foot back on the shaft and it didn't stall, but it did shudder a bit, shudder, and then he tightened his grip on the wheel and just went slowly, slowly down the road, past the houses, most of them lit up as it got dark, past the mouth of the Horn Creek road, to the flat space where the Eureka Pipeline gauging station used to be— where he had worked for so many years, after goddamn Eureka pulled him out of Grantsville and back to Burnt House, the station torn down now and hauled away, just a weedy muddy flat space with some oil drums and busted machinery, and Talbot felt tired right then. The years felt heavy, 87 goddamn years. None of them worth anything at all now. That goddamn boy won. Couldn't drive the car to Morgantown with that pedal missing. Goddamn it to hell. That goddamn boy fucked everything up. That goddamn boy sabotaged me.

Talbot pulled over at the gauging station—tried to pull over—but that damn shaft, he pushed too hard on it this time or something and the car lurched ahead and shot through the puddles into the brush, into a patch of multiflora rose all gray and brown and dead in the winter—and almost through and damn near into the creek before he got stopped.

Talbot thought, Goddamn.

I can't do it.

Almost 70 years of driving a car and now that's over. Can't even drive a car now! Used to drive everywhere. Drove trucks over those hills. Through the mud. Corduroy roads. Cars. Ox teams. Horses. Mules. Drove every goddamn thing everywhere you could drive.

Talbot put the car in reverse and tried to back slowly out of the brush. Tried—again he punched the shaft too hard with his big foot and the car shot back across the lot into a couple of rusted oil drums and they banged over loud as hell.

Son of a bitch.

The light went on at Davis's house across the road. Davis came out and stood in his doorway and watched.

Talbot took a breath. Blinked, took another breath. He put the car slowly—carefully, carefully, he thought— into drive, and slowly, slowly, lowered his foot down onto the wire, and the car moved—slowly too—and he pulled back onto the goddamn road. He drove back up through town. Past Butchie's store, and now both Claudie and Butchie were standing out there watching him go past. Talbot pretended to ignore them, drove straight past the schoolhouse and the church, past the old Langford house, looking straight ahead. Past Ellyson's. Driving a damn car. His own damn car, past his own goddamn house, and he saw he'd forgotten to put his own porch light on, the house dark, dark, and he drove on up the road to Page's store, circling around there, his foot slipping off the shaft when he turned the wheel—and the wheel itself was stiff and hard to turn, and the car shot wide and lurched again, this time swinging clear over by the post office, almost hitting Bess's pickup truck but not quite hitting it, and rolling back down the road again. To home. Pulled back in front of the garage, off the road, stopped. Took a deep breath.

Turned off the car.

That's all over now, he thought. It's all over. That's all over. Everything's over.

God damn.

I'm all over.

Across the yard, in the house, the kitchen light came on. That damn boy. That damn Mark. That wasted fuck. Finally coming up and getting something to eat. And— yes, then the boy came into the kitchen. Talbot could see him through the window, even across the yard. Inside there moving around, standing in front of the stove, eating, eating, the fat worthless son of a bitch. Talbot watched him for a long time, sitting in the still car, and the evening got darker and darker, and cold.

Later Died

Many times I'd hear an old-timer end a story with two words: "Later died." And then they'd nod, and look at me, and the silence would build, and I wouldn't even ask what happened next, because the story was obviously over. There wasn't anything much left to say. The rest of the life of the person in the story didn't matter much, this person who'd been in a car wreck, or shot a big deer, or said something funny, this person who lived and later died.

Later died.

And that's all there was to them!

So there.

We'll all come to it someday.

So. Gran had a friend from church, Mrs. Pearl Reed, and Mrs. Reed had a granddaughter named Fayette, and Fayette was having a birthday, and she wanted a party. And because of Gran, Liza and myself were invited.

It was the summer of 1968, and I was five years old, and I didn't want to go. But, right, I was five years old, and my vote didn't count for much. Nobody cared what I wanted. Gran dressed us in our church clothes and drove us to Mrs. Reed's house and dropped us off.

At five I was one of the youngest children at the party, and the ages of the others ranged up to about twelve or thirteen—Ace Everett was there, Alan Charles Everett, Ace, and he was about three years older than Liza, which would have made him thirteen. My cousin Mark was down from Minnesota that summer, was at the party, and he was eleven or twelve. Most of the kids were younger than that.

My memory of that day is too fragmented and faint to conform to a real narrative—as I think it over, the day becomes a series of images and feelings, up to what happened at the end. I remember I was dressed up and mad, and I didn't want to be there, and none of the other girls would talk to me, or maybe I wouldn't talk to them. That's not a story, that's a statement. I know that at some point I got bored with hanging around the shady yard eating sticky sweet cake, and I wandered down the hill to watch the boys fishing off the bridge.

It was a hot day, and sunny and still, and Horn Creek was muddy under the bridge. Weeping willows lined the banks, branches trailing in the water.

I think I was always a little shy and skittish around strangers, around boys, and I stayed on the edge of the bridge, the end closest to the house, and watched. Mark and Ace were fishing, along with a couple of other boys I don't remember and probably didn't know. They were fishing with bait and bobbers, and the red-and-white bobbers were floating up next to the willows.

There was a sign on the road just before you came to the bridge that said FALLING ROCK—a common sign along roads all over West Virginia. Here, at Mrs. Reed's, after the road crossed the bridge heading toward Burnt House, it curved and cut into the side of the hill, and a high rock wall rose up. Mrs. Reed's house was on little rise, a flat place well back from the creek and the road, set back under some big, shady trees. A nice spot for a house: even after Mrs. Reed's old house burned down in the 1990s—well after Mrs. Reed herself later died, of course—someone put a double-wide trailer up there. I drove by this spot hundreds of times over the years, but I never stopped by there again after that day in 1968.

Anyway. The boys were fishing, and Mark's bobber moved a little bit. Mark yanked at the line but didn't hook a fish.

That's a gar, Ace said. I know he said something about a gar. I remember that because I wasn't sure what a gar was. (Turns out it's a big, ugly fish with a lot of teeth).

Mark said, There's no gars in here.

Maybe there was already some sort of tension between the boys. I don't know or I don't remember. But they started arguing about gars—Ace said there were gars in the creek, Mark said there weren't. It went back and forth, and I was alarmed—wondering, maybe, where the grownups were, wondering which one of those boys was going to get a whipping—and then Ace grabbed Mark's fishing pole to catch a gar and prove himself right.

Mark wouldn't let go.

They had a brief, violent tussle. Ace was a little older and a little bigger, but Mark was mad and he wouldn't let go. Then Ace tripped—or was tripped—and went down hard on his back, right on the hot asphalt road.

Whoa!

I figured somebody was going to get in trouble. Not me, though. I took a step back.

Right then I saw an older boy named Milty coming down the road, coming along under the rocky road cut.

He was carrying a rifle.

I knew Milty a little bit—he was Mrs. Reed's nephew or something, his name was Milton, everyone called him Milty, and Gran had hired him a time or two to cut the brush along the creek in front of our house and to do little jobs. He was, I guess, 18 or so then, vastly older it seemed, though still not a real grownup like Gran or my dad. As for the rifle—I guess now he'd been out shooting groundhogs in the meadows; I don't know what I knew at the time. Probably nothing. I just knew he was coming back toward us carrying a rifle over his shoulder, shirtless and tanned in the summer sun.

I'd never seen a real rifle before. I clung close to the bridge abutment.

Ace was still on his back on the pavement, and then he saw Milty coming, too. He scrambled to his feet and took off running to meet him. He pointed back at Mark and screamed, "Kill him! Kill him!"

Just looking at those words on the page does not in any way capture the sound or power they had that day at the bridge. I've mostly avoided depicting accents in these stories but they were always there to a greater or lesser extent, and Ace that day had the traditional long diphthong on "kill"— "*keee-yul*" exaggerated in his anger.

"Keee-yul him! Keee-yul him!" Loud and shrill and full of rage.

But Milty didn't kill Mark. He just laughed and showed his white teeth. He said, "Aw, I'm not going to kill anybody."

Ace sputtered, "But—but—"

And then Milty put his hand on Ace's head and pushed him away—not hard at all, but Ace tripped over his own feet and sat down hard on his butt.

Everybody laughed.

And so Mark stood his ground and won the day, with a little help.

Milty went on up to the house, and as he passed me he said, "Hey, little Jackie."

I don't think I ever saw him again. He was drafted that year and sent to Vietnam—and, sadly, later died.

Sleep Enough

The old man never went to bed early enough.

He'd sit and stare at the TV, watching all through the evening, through the news and on into Johnny Carson, grumping and arguing about everything, making everyone miserable. This went on for months and months, until one evening when Mark got fed up and decided to knock the old bastard out.

That night Brandy called and said she could maybe sneak over later, but it really would be sneaking, because her parents didn't want her going out, and the old man didn't like her hanging around, either. She could come over only after everyone was asleep, and her parents had just now gone to bed, and her little sister, too, and what was *wrong* with that old man? Why didn't he just go to sleep like everybody else?

"He's too mean to sleep," Mark said.

"I bet he is," Brandy said.

"He has nightmares when he does sleep," Mark said.

"I'm not surprised, he's so mean."

The phone was a party line, anybody could listen in if they wanted to. Mark didn't care, though, he wanted everyone to know how mean the old man was.

"He wakes up screaming in the night, sometimes,"

Mark said. "He says things chase him in his sleep."

"Good!" Brandy said. Then she lowered her voice. Whispered. "Don't you want to see me?"

Mark paused. The phone was in the dining room and the old man was out there in the front room sitting in his wheelchair in front of the TV. He'd grumped a little when Mark came in to talk on the phone, but no more than usual. "Don't worry, Pap, it's not long distance," Mark told him. Long distance made the old man crazy.

Just about everything made the old man crazy.

"Don't you?" Brandy asked.

"Sure," Mark said. Party line or no.

"He needs to get to sleep!" Brandy said. "What's his problem?"

The dining room door bumped open then and the old man came scooting in.

"You still talking to that girl?"

"Still talking," Mark said.

"What?" Brandy asked. "Is that him? Is he there?"

"Yeah...."

"I wish he'd just go to sleep!"

The old man hoisted himself up and out of the chair and took a clumsy, awkward step or two into the kitchen. It was painful to watch him—it hurt. The old bastard moved so slow. Mark heard a pan bang into something against the stove. Then something clattered hitting the floor. Another pan. Mark thought, I'd like to hit him over the head with a pan and knock him out.

Then he thought—Well. *Well.* I could maybe—I could knock him out. Maybe. Could.

Mark said into the phone, "Call me back."

It was his brother Paul's idea—Paul had actually done it first, done it a lot of times, at least he said he had. Bragged. He'd been a medic in the Green Berets, he knew about medicine and pills, he spent a summer once in Burnt House after he got out of the army. "When that old man starts acting up and cussing at me like a dog, I just dump some pills in his coffee and knock him the fuck out," Paul said. "It always works." Mark remembered thinking—No, that's not right, to slip Pap a pill like that. A handful of pills. That might kill Pap! It seemed wrong to Mark, but that was before he moved to Burnt House himself and found out what a true bastard the old man really was. Now—now it made sense.

Mark hung up the phone and went out through the front room—Johnny Carson's monologue was over and he was sitting at the desk with Ed—and then went down to the basement, to his bedroom. After his Grammaw had died, Mark took all her potentially useful prescriptions— Dilaudid, Tylenol 3, Valium—and put them in a box hidden away on a shelf in his room, and no one, not even Brandy, knew he had them. Mark pulled the box down and the Valium looked like it might work. One or two, though? One? Two? Or maybe three?

"One," Mark said aloud. He didn't know, though. The old man was skinny—and old—and two might be too many.

One might be too many, too, Mark thought—but what the hell.

The old bastard needed to sleep, anyway. Maybe he needed to sleep forever.

No, really—he *did* need to sleep forever.

Two pills. Or three.

Back upstairs the old man was still messing around in the kitchen. The damn wheelchair was blocking the doorway, and Mark couldn't get around it to see what was going on.

"Pap?" Mark asked. "What're you doing in there?"

"I'm looking for—" the old man banged into something else. "Hell, I don't know. Looking to get something to eat, I guess."

"Well, get out of the way, Pap. I'll see if I can find you something."

The old man came back around the corner of the stove

and lowered himself heavily into the wheelchair.

"I don't know," the old man said. "I can't find any goddamn thing in there."

Mark scrunched around him and stood by the sink. The old man looked alert and mean sitting there, pale and skinny with the kitchen light glinting off his glasses. The evil goddamn son of a bitch piece of shit.

"Maybe some hot chocolate?" Mark asked. "Some hot chocolate and maybe a piece of that cake? Maybe that'll help you sleep."

"Hell, I guess."

Mark poured some milk in a pan and set it on the fire, low. He went further back in the kitchen so the old man couldn't see and crushed up a pair of the little pale blue tablets, and then he brought the powder back and dumped it into the milk. It didn't bubble or anything. That was probably good. But was it enough? Too much? When the milk was warm, he poured it out in a cup and then added a package of hot chocolate mix. It looked okay.

Mark stuck his head around the corner and looked in the dining room. The old man was just sitting in his wheelchair staring at the table. Just staring. Not even doing anything. What was he thinking about?

Ways to treat people bad, probably.

"Go on out and look at the TV," Mark said. "I'll bring it to you."

The old man wheeled out and went into the front room. Mark sliced a piece of Mary's chocolate cake and brought it and the hot chocolate out to the old man.

"Here you go," Mark said.

The old man grunted and squinted down into the cup.

"It's not too hot, I don't think," Mark said.

The old man sipped his drink and they watched Johnny Carson talking with Mary Tyler Moore. It was hot in the room—it was always hot—and the fire was showing blue and yellow flames.

After a while the old man yawned.

"Getting sleepy?" Mark asked.

"Goddamn it to hell," the old man said.

Mark was holding a copy of the Weston paper, pretending to read it while the old man yawned and nodded. After a while, he did read it a little—there was a court listing for a man named Simon Posey, from Old Field Fork, who'd been sentenced for burglary. Brandy's mother was a Posey, from over in Lewis County. The Posey's had a reputation for being a trashy bunch, though Mark had once heard the old man allow that not all the Posey's were bad. Maybe he was talking about Brandy— she wasn't bad. The old man didn't much like her, though. But then he didn't much like anybody.

Now the old man sighed and scooted his chair to the door of his bedroom, and he pulled himself up by the doorframe and took a wobbly step or two over to the bed and sat down. The TV was still playing. Dick Van Dyke came out and sat with Johnny and Mary. Everybody on the TV was happy.

"Are you through watching, Pap?" Mark asked.

"Hell, I don't know." The old man kicked off his slippers and slowly lowered himself back into bed. He reached up and shut off the light.

Mark waited for a moment. Then he got up and walked into the dining room and called Brandy—called her number, her parents' number—and let it ring once. Then he hung up. Their signal.

Back in the front room, Mark turned off the TV and stood outside the old man's room. Asleep, at last. Really, it was a good thing, to sleep. A few days earlier the old man had been complaining about being tired, about not getting sleep—he said back when he was young and working hard he needed nine hours or so of sleep a night. Now he was down to two or three. Tired all the damn time, he said—and, really, he was sick and wasted away and skinnied down to nothing but meanness and bone and meanness and bone and anger. Rage. Almost ninety years of being mad. But now he was sleeping. Sleeping.

Maybe he was sleeping.

There were soft steps on the front porch and Brandy stuck her head in the door. Mark gestured silence and waved her in the direction of the kitchen and he followed her. The old man was quiet in his room.

"He's asleep?" Brandy whispered.

"He just dropped off." Mark stood in the doorway watching Brandy. She was busily putting away all the cans of food and cooking pots the old man had pulled down and left sitting out. She was quiet, though, working with her lips pursed. Mark said, "We'd better be quiet for a little bit."

"That mean old man," Brandy said. "Still, you have to be nice to him."

Mark said, "I wish he was dead half the time."

Brandy jumped and kissed at him—awkward, she missed his mouth or he flinched and she banged her nose into this cheek. They both laughed.

"Don't be down on yourself," Brandy said. "You're a good grandson! Look how you take care of that old man. Look how you take care of me."

"Yeah," Mark said. He thought, I took care of the son of a bitch, all right. Maybe I'll kill him. Maybe I'd like to kill him. I sure drugged him. Those two pills. "I suppose."

"Yeah," Brandy said. She put her arms around his waist. "And we're going to have a good life together when you go, right?"

"Sure."

"Sure?" Brandy asked.

She kept asking that. Mark thought she didn't sound so sure, sometimes.

"Yeah. Sure." Mark hugged her back, a little, he smelled the lilac shampoo in her hair, the traces of smoke on her jacket. On the shelf behind her Mark saw cans of pork and beans stacked up. The old man liked his goddamn pork and beans. The old man always got what he wanted.

Mark said, "We'll have fun. And he'll die someday."

They kissed quickly and broke apart. Mark shut off the kitchen light and then took Brandy's hand and led her through the dining room, and shut off the light there, and out into the front room. He let go of Brandy and shut off the lamp by the television. There was a night-light glowing from the old man's room, and Brandy stepped as softly as she could across the squeaking floor and stood in his doorway, outlined in the soft blue light. Mark watched her stand there for a moment, the ends of her hair almost glowing, the rough fabric of her jean jacket, and he stepped next to her and put his hand at the small of her back. The denim was cool.

"He's not dead, right?" Brandy whispered.

The old man lay on his side, facing them. Skinny like a skeleton, his teeth were in but his glasses were off, and his eyes shut as if he really were dead in the blue glow. He wasn't moving at all.

"Mark?" Brandy leaned back into him, softly. "You sure he's okay?"

No, Mark thought, no—he's not okay.

He's never been okay, the son of a bitch.

He's never had an okay day in his goddamn life.

The old man gasped then—shuddered, shivered, slowly inhaled.

Alive, still.

Brandy backed up, pushing Mark away from the doorway, and he took her arm and led her around to the hallway and they started down the stairs to the basement, to his bedroom.

"Kill me if I ever get like that," Mark said over his shoulder.

"Aw, baby," Brandy said. She touched the back of Mark's head. "You're never going to get like that."

Part Three
Do It or Have It Done

Some Ways that People End Up

Butchie Randolph was always kind of a mess, fat and dirty from working on cars, sitting outside his store and scratching and smoking and watching people go up and down the road. But Page Westfall—and Page's store, too— was quite different. Page wore his shirt tucked-in and his store goods were new and stacked in some sort of order, and his store was clean. Page was always a big talker, too. I remember one time years later I went back for the holidays and stopped in and he gave a hoot.

"There's that Stalnaker girl, her hair's all in a curl."

Well, my hair's always been more or less straight, and anyway I was wearing a hoody that day to keep the chill off my ears. But whatever. Page was still glad to see me, glad to see almost everybody, full of news and gossip—who was in the hospital, who had bought a new car, and even—based on his sales of toilet paper and Pepto Bismol—who in the community had diarrhea that Sunday.

"I don't know if I want to hear about that," I said.

"Oh, people are sick," Page said. He sounded like he cared. But maybe he did care! Maybe the old gossip-monger really did care. I don't know. He said, "There's something going around. Something bad."

I still didn't want to hear about it. I looked around

the store. Facing the door, right next to the cash register, was the mounted head of a black bear. There was a stove off to the right, and a bench with a couple of old-timers sitting on it, Gid Ellyson and Dayton Davis, but it was that bear head that caught my eye. There was a brass tag on the wooden base that said Webster County 1964. I realized then I'd been looking at that bear head for years and years—for all my life, really—but I never had known how it got there.

"You know," I said, "I don't think you ever told me how you shot that bear."

Hearing about the bear might be better than hearing about whoever was running off at the bowels. Would be better.

"Well," Page said. "Well, well, well." He came around the counter and stood in front of the bear head, and stared at it, thoughtful and silent for a moment. Then he sat down on the wooden bench between the two old men.

"Well, now, that's a simple story," Page said. "And you already know how it ended."

"The bear later died," I said. "Yeah."

Page was an erect little man but he sat up a little straighter, even. "Well, now, Maud"—his wife, Maud—"she's from up in Webster County, and her brother, Henry, he keeps bear hounds, or he did keep bear hounds. He used to go bear hunting every year up there. You ever seen those mountains?"

"I've been through there," I said.

"That's some rugged country up in those mountains. Those people are rugged, too."

"Ol' Maud's sure rugged," old-timer Dayton Davis said. He sort of snickered. A joke.

"Oh, she is!" Page said. No joke to him. "Maud's a strong woman! Maud works like a man!"

"Some men hardly work at all," Gid Ellyson said. Was that a joke? Gid was one of the laziest men around. "Or they try not to."

"The bears...." I said.

"And—Henry kept those bear dogs," Page said. "And so one Thanksgiving we went bear hunting, and those dogs chased that bear down one mountain and over the next, and they treed it, and I shot the son of a bitch. Put his head right there on my wall."

Page nodded. So there.

I nodded back. So there!

But I waited, too. That was all? He shot the bear? The bear later died? It wasn't much of a story. There had to be more to the dead bear head than that.

"Well?" I finally asked.

"Well, what?"

"I always heard bear meat's greasy," Gid said.

"What else happened to the bear?" I asked. I was expecting some sort of tale where the bear came down from the tree and fought it out with ol' Henry's dogs and Page had to stab the bear with his Barlow knife. Something dramatic like that.

"That's what happened to the bear, right there!" Page pointed to the snarling bear head.

"I hear you can get that trichinosis from eating a bear," Dayton said.

"The bear died," Page said. "You already know the ending of that story. How come you want to hear a story when you already know how it ends?"

Gid shook his head. "I don't want to eat no greasy bear meat."

"Now listen, Jackie—I'm asking you a question," Page said to me.

"Well...." I shrugged like I didn't know—well, but then I did know, sort of, and do. There are some books I can read over and over, some movies I can see again and again, some music I can listen to forever and ever. Not all, or even a lot, but some, and with every repetition the meaning grows and grows and sometimes changes. And then, too, sometimes you have to find out how to get to the end of something two or three or five or ten times to understand what the end means or even if it really is the end.

"And what about all these outlaws around here?" Page asked.

"What? Outlaws?" And here I thought we were talking about bears, or stories.

Outlaws?

"Hell, yes!" Page got up and stalked back around the store's counter. The two old men sitting on the bench nodded. So there. Hell, yes.

Again I stood and waited for the story.

"You know that ol' Jackson boy who never wears a shirt? They call him Naked Jackson?"

"That boy never wears a shirt," Gid Ellyson said.

"Even deer hunting he never wears a shirt!" Dayton Davis said. "Who ever heard of that?"

"Cold out there in deer season."

"Well, he's back in the penitentiary now," Page said. "They'll make him wear a shirt in there, I'll bet."

"He'll get one of those striped shirts," Gid said.

"What'd they get him on?" I asked. I subscribed to the county paper all the time I was in college, but I'd never seen anything about Naked Jackson.

"Oh, that dope," Page said. Like it was boring. That dope. He didn't even bother to nod. "It's all the same—all these Jacksons, all these Cottrells, all these Baileys—they're all just a bunch of damn outlaws."

"Not all those Baileys are bad," Dayton said.

"Well, there's Bailey's and there's Baileys," Gid said. "They're sort of like the Poseys like that."

"That's why you can never trust a Bailey or a Posey," Dayton said. "Bad or not, you'll never know."

"And that's the whole darn point!" Page was getting excited. He banged his hand on the counter. "That's the whole point! You never know which of these filthy youngins will grow up to be bad, and which ones won't. They're all stories that don't have endings! Now, you know I'm right, Jackie."

Again I thought, What? I said, "Well...."

"Now, you see I know!" Page banged his hand on the counter again. "Some of those kids will grow up to be bad—but then some of them, they'll start going to church, and some of them others will get tired of being bad and settle down, and some of them will move away—and some of them will steal the battery right out of your truck, or try to sell you dope!"

Page took a deep breath, and the old-timers nodded— see, now, they knew, so there—and the dead bear's glass eyes glittered and I stood and waited for all the stories to come.

As Worthless as Anyone Else

By spring, Brandy and Liza were back being friends again. One evening, after she got off work at the Foodland in Glenville, Brandy drove back up through the college, where Liza was waiting at the campus bookstore for a ride back to Burnt House. Brandy found her standing just inside the door, talking to a couple of boys. She honked the horn. After another minute or so, Liza came on out and got in the car.

"You took long enough," Brandy said.

"You took longer," Liza said. "I've been waiting, I don't know—hours, at least."

"Waiting won't hurt you any," Brandy said. "Anyway—you wouldn't believe what Ronnie had me doing today." Ronnie was the manager at the Foodland, a fat baloony snob. "He wanted me to mop the floors! He wanted me to take out the trash! Wanted me to clean the whole store! He thinks he's so important, bossing me around like that."

"Yeah, he's awful big-feeling," Liza said. "Hey—let's go by Naked's, see what he's doing."

Brandy shook her head but didn't say anything. Naked Jackson. Liza was supposed to be broke up with him again. But still Brandy drove down the hill and through town and then up Sycamore Run. She slowed a bit when she got to Naked's trailer.

"His truck's not here," Brandy said.

"Nope," Liza said. She craned around in her seat, looking over the trailer as they passed. "I didn't think it would be."

"Then why—"

"Maybe he's over at Ace's," Liza said. "We should probably stop there."

"I don't know," Brandy said. "I think I should probably get home."

"You hate going home!" Liza was laughing. "You hate going home but you're always in a hurry to get back to Burnt House. You're just really crazy. You know you are."

"No," Brandy said. But—no. That was true, sort of: Brandy did hate going home. There was nothing there except people being mad all the time. Mom, Daddy, Jessica, all of them mad about something all the time and arguing and complaining. Daddy gone a lot and half the time threatening to not ever come back, which would be a good thing, but it was mostly all big talk because he always did come back, sick and drunk and mad. There wasn't any place else for him to go. There wasn't any place else at all, it seemed like, for any of them. Daddy should have left a long time ago, taken them all along so they could live decent, but now it was too late and they were all stuck in Burnt House hating each other. And Mark—it wasn't too different over at the Talbot's. Brandy would go over there to see Mark, and Old Man Talbot would gripe and grouch and pout and be hateful to everybody. He lived in that house 60 years or more and it got him nothing but being mad. He should have moved on, too—he even said so, once, he said he should have moved to Weirton and worked in the steel mills, he should have moved to Detroit and built cars. But he stayed in Burnt House, like a damn fool, and spent his time being mad at people. But Mark—Mark wasn't a fool. Mark was going to leave. Mark wasn't going to stay in Burnt House.

"It won't take long to stop by there," Liza said. "And it's on the way home, too."

"What?" Oh—Ace's place. Liza wanted to get high. Of course.

"You won't be late," Liza said.

Brandy thought of her mother getting mad about taking so long to get home from work, like it was any of her business. I can't stand that, Brandy thought, people talking and spying and gossiping, watching each other like a hawk.

"It's not right," Brandy said.

"Huh?" Liza asked. "What?"

"Nothing."

And that Ace Everett, he was just like all the other boys she knew—stupid. Good for nothing. Worthless, all of them. All the men—the ones who drove slowly up and down the road in their pickups, the ones who sat around loafing at Butchie's store or Page's store, the ones in town who pretended to go to college, or sold dope. Her daddy, too. And her uncles. All worthless. Old Man Talbot was smart and he'd worked hard and he'd saved a lot of money, but he was so mean he was worthless, a worthless mean old miser. Mark was different, though— he was smart, too, like the old man, and he worked hard, but even though his mom was from Burnt House, he'd grown up in Minnesota, and so he was different. Smart and sweet, not worthless, not greedy, he'd been to a real college, he was going to do something with his life once he got away from that old man. Poor Mark, he just didn't get how worthless and stupid everyone else in Burnt House was. Once, she'd tried to explain how her daddy had lost his eye and dropped the baby off the roof at the same time and busted the baby's head, but it was frustrating.

"He was up on the roof working and a nail hit him," Brandy said.

"A *nail* hit him?" Mark asked, amazed. He was so out of it, sometimes. Smart but still not knowing. "How did a nail hit him in the eye?"

"I don't know," Brandy said. "I wasn't up there, too. All I know is a nail hit him in the eye, and they had the baby up there—"

"The *baby*? On the *roof*?"

"Yeah," Brandy said. The baby—her little cousin Jojo. They dropped him off the roof and busted his little head. Brandy took a deep breath. Sighed. It was almost too hard to explain. "See, they was all up there on the roof with the baby, and they was all drunk, and they're just all *stupid*!"

Mark looked at her, appalled.

It made her mad, that look. Stupid innocent superior look. But at least Mark wasn't worthless, he was going to take her along when he left Burnt House, he wasn't anything like Ace Everett or Naked Jackson or her daddy or her uncles or any of the others, who were all worthless with nothing to look forward to but smoking dope and living up some holler somewhere and raising chickens and going on welfare or whatever.

"Aw, just nothing," Brandy said again to Liza. "Nothing's right."

Ace lived in a pale brown trailer wedged in a holler off of Sleeth Run. Naked's truck wasn't out front, but Ace's old Chevy Nova was there, and Brandy parked behind it and the girls got out and went up the steps. Liza banged on the door, and after a minute or so Ace stuck his shaggy head out.

"What?" Ace asked. Then, "Oh."

"We came looking for Naked," Liza said. "Thought we'd say hello."

"Well," Ace said. He opened the door and let the girls in. "He was here, now he's somewhere else."

Liza sat down on the couch and Brandy sat next to her. Across the small room a television with the sound turned off was tuned to the Mr. Cartoon show, and next to the TV was an aquarium with guppies and goldfish floating around the water with a real-looking human skull. Ace sank down into a sagging chair, looking tired.

"You girls looking for something?" Ace asked.

"Maybe," Liza said. "Looking for Naked, at least."

Ace brought out some weed and some papers and rolled up a joint, and then another.

"Never know where people are going," Ace said. "Naked, he left here a while ago."

Ace always sounded kind of stupid and bad-tempered—and maybe he was kind of stupid and bad-tempered. People said he was afraid of girls, that he might be a homo, but sometimes he'd be around and he'd smile at her with his surprising white teeth, smiled like he was sweet and sick at the same time. Whatever he was, he was as worthless as anybody else. He wasn't going to do anything with his life. Brandy never wanted to be around him unless she had to. He was Naked's friend, and Naked was Liza's boyfriend, at least some of the time. The pot passed around, and Ace talked about his mother's cat that got hit by a car and died and how they were all sad, they'd had that cat such a long time, and he talked about some guy Brandy didn't know who broke off with his girlfriend and got drunk and drove his car into a tree, and he talked about how he went to Clarksburg last week, and Liza talked about Naked some, and she talked about her classes at Glenville State, and a couple more joints went around. Brandy only half-listened. Ace and Liza were both big talkers, they acted like they knew something nobody else knew, something secret and all important, and knowing things made them big. Brandy's daddy was like that, too. A lot of people were, they thought they were big. "Ford Mustang—*1965* Ford Mustang—is the best car ever made," they'd say, for example—and Daddy said stupid shit like that all the time—and then the big talker would *nod*. That nod—that was the sign that they knew the secret, that the big talker was important, that you couldn't argue against them. Just about everybody did it, all the men, some of the women, all the big talkers—Old Man Talbot, Ace, Butchie at the store, Page at his store, everybody. "Now, you see I *know*," Daddy would say, and nod. And he never knew a damn thing, ever, not even when he was sober. None of them ever knew anything, all talking so big. Just look at that Ace, Brandy thought, thinking about him and trying to ignore him at the same time. Big talker, and he's got nothing worth talking about.

"You ever see Dan Morris shoot a rifle?" Ace asked. Brandy didn't even know who Dan Morris was. Or care. Ace said, "He can dot an *I* on a printed page at three-hundred yard." The nod. "Three-hundred yard. I stepped it off myself."

Nod.

"Wow," Liza said. She was stoned.

But—Brandy realized—she was stoned, too. Oh shit, she thought. Oh well. She was really only half-listening, and maybe even that was too much since the big talkers weren't saying anything worth hearing. She looked at the TV with the sound turned off—Mr. Cartoon showing a Bugs Bunny, Elmer chasing Bugs. Just like everything else in the world but Bugs would be okay. Elmer was stupid like all those men. He knew it all. He was another worthless nodder. In the aquarium next to the TV, a little catfish came swimming out the eye-hole of that ugly wet skull and nosed around a bit and went swimming back inside the skull.

"Man," Brandy suddenly said. "That skull's freaking me out."

Liza and Ace stopped talking and looked at the tank.

"Why do you even *have* that thing?" Brandy asked.

"It's a decoration," Liza said. "I guess."

"It's a real skull, too," Ace said.

"No!" Liza said.

"Off a real human being," Ace said. He nodded. "Off an old dead lady."

Nod.

So there.

Brandy had been sliding slouching down on the couch, stoned, but now she sat up straight, shrinking back from the damn skull. What an ignorant big-talker. A skull in the fish tank. A real skull. A real old lady's skull. Disgusting.

"That's not real," Liza said. "How'd you go and get a real skull?"

"Found it," Ace said. Nod. "Over on Laurel Run. You know that cemetery up there? Part of it must've washed away in the high water last winter."

"No way," Brandy said.

"Found a bunch of old bones," Ace said. "Only that one skull, though."

"What were you doing up there?" Brandy asked.

"I found some arm bones, found some ribs—"

"Stop!" Liza said. "I don't want to hear this!"

"There was some skin on that skull," Ace said. He flashed a smile, strong white teeth in his stupid stoned face. "Had some hair on it, too. So I brought it home, put it in a bucket of water and boiled it down—"

"Stop!" Liza covered her ears.

"—boiled it right down." Ace nodded.

"You're making me sick," Liza said.

"Made it clean."

"Stop," Brandy said.

Ace sat there smiling, lank brown hair framing his face. It was just big talk to him—showed how important he was, with some old dead lady's skull in his fish tank. Somebody's old dead grammaw. The room was silent for a moment and they all stared stoned at the skull and listened to the tank bubble. The guppies and goldfish floated around and did their fish things, and then the little catfish came careening out an eyehole again. Brandy looked away.

"Ow!" Liza yelled. "No!"

"I hate that thing," Brandy said.

Ace sat back looking pleased.

"We have to go," Brandy said. "I have to get home."

The girls ended up buying a half-once of weed and they trooped out to the car and got in. Ace stood in the doorway of the trailer, smiling at them, leaning against the doorjamb, his arms crossed in front of his chest. Brandy thought he looked like he was about to nod, the big-feeling rat.

"I was getting freaked out in there," Liza said.

"He thinks he's so big," Brandy said. She started the car and shifted into reverse, and then stopped. "Shit," she said. "I hate to drive through town all stoned like this—the cops'll see us."

Liza thought. "Well, just go over the top of the hill, here." She pointed up the road past Ace's trailer. "This comes out on Alice Road. We'll be almost home."

"It'll be all muddy," Brandy said. Ace was still leaning in the doorway, all high-looking, staring at them. "We'll get bogged down."

"It's fine," Liza said. "I drive it all the time."

"You do not!" Brandy said. "Your mom never lets you drive her car."

"When I sneak out I drive this road all the time!"

"You do not," Brandy said. But she went ahead and backed the car out of Ace's driveway, not looking up at Ace, and she didn't go back through town but headed up over the hill. She was aware she was loaded, really loaded, high, stoned, and she drove slowly with both hands on the wheel. Trees closed in around the car but the road itself wasn't too bad, mostly gravel with a few muddy spots going up through the woods. Brandy had a cassette deck in the car, and Liza fumbled around with the tapes and then stuck Peter Frampton's live album in and turned up the sound. Brandy thought it sounded worse loud on her blown-out speakers but she drove slowly on and they came out along the top of a ridge with woods above them on the right but a view to the left of well-fed cows grazing in pastures with more woods in the distance, and more woods, and hills.

"This is the Westfall place," Liza said over the music. "You know that Danny Westfall?"

Brandy thought for a moment. "I know Sara."

"Yeah, Danny's little sister," Liza said. She made it her business to know everyone. "This is their cousin's place. This is a nice farm. They got some money."

Then they were back in the woods again. Brandy gripped the wheel tight, focusing. Driving. Stoned. Trying to stay in the road. Frampton wanted to know if she felt like he did, and she figured she probably didn't. When they came to wet places in the road, Brandy slowed up even more and eased the car through the mud.

"You need to speed up," Liza said. "You need to hit that mud fast and just get through it!"

"No!" That was crazy. Slow through mud holes— that's what old man Talbot said, and for once he probably knew what he was talking about, he drove trucks over the muddy mountains working in the oil fields all those years. "That's crazy."

"Go faster!" Liza said. "That's the way I always drive this road!"

"You do not," Brandy said. Even if she did, it was stupid. "Elizabeth Marie, you're such a liar."

"What?"

Just then a jeep came barreling around the curve straight at them down the middle of the road. Brandy hit the brakes and Liza screamed and the car swerved over into the shallow ditch and thudded up against the bank. The jeep skidded past them and then stopped back down the road.

"Oh," Brandy gasped. She held onto the steering wheel and stared straight ahead. "Oh."

"Damn," Liza said. She craned around and looked out the back. "That's little Kenny Woofter."

Brandy saw that the Frampton cassette was halfway out of the deck. Must have ejected itself. The car was off, too. Did it turn itself off? Brandy didn't remember switching it off. Behind, the jeep reversed and backed up until driver's window was opposite Brandy's. He was just a kid. Brandy rolled down her window.

"I'm sorry!" Kenny Woofter said.

Liza leaned across Brandy. "You about killed us!" she said. "You need to watch where you're going!"

"I'm sorry!" Kenny Woofter said again. "I was just out practicing...." He was only a kid. Eyes wide and mouth slack and lips wet.

"Wow," Brandy said. She shook her head. Crazy. She didn't even remember turning the car off, unless it turned itself off. No matter. She shifted into park and turned the key and it started right up. She pulled the transmission into drive and the car gave a little lurch but didn't go anywhere, and when she pushed the gas the wheels just spit leaves and mud. Little Kenny Woofter just sat in his jeep staring open-mouthed. Worthless as any grown man.

"We're stuck," Brandy said. "Damn."

Liza leaned over Brandy out the window. "Kenny, get out and push."

"He can't push us out," Brandy said. "He's too little."

"Uh," Kenny said. "I'll go get my dad—he's got a winch on his pickup."

"That's great," Brandy said. She just sat staring up the muddy road to where it curved into the trees.

"Well, hurry up!" Liza said. "We've got places to be!"

Kenny backed his jeep up and made an eight-point turn to get around and head back to his home.

"Worthless stupid," Brandy said. Stupid! Worthless.

"He's okay," Liza said. "He's only fourteen? Fifteen? He's young."

"He's an idiot."

Liza settled back in her seat and pulled a joint from inside her shirt and lit it. "Might as well have some fun," she said.

"Some fun." Brandy inhaled. "All these boys around here are so stupid."

Smoke was filling the car despite Brandy's open window. Liza rolled down her window, too. She said, "Some of them I guess are."

"Okay," Brandy said. "Here's an idea. I was thinking last night I might want to get pregnant."

Liza coughed, stared at Brandy. "What?"

"Yep," Brandy said. She took a hit off the joint and passed it to Liza.

"No—really? You don't want a baby."

"Maybe not," Brandy said. She exhaled. "I don't know. But I'm thinking maybe Mark would take me with him for sure if I have a baby, right?"

"No!" Liza said. "He'll run away, is what he'll do."

Brandy didn't say anything. She sat there looking straight ahead, waiting to get pulled out of the mud.

A Ghost Town

One summer afternoon when I was 12 or so I was over at the Talbots sitting with Grammaw Talbot out on the porch, just visiting. Across the road and down a little, about halfway between the Talbot's and Butchie's store, was an old house set up above the road a bit. The old house was unpainted, dilapidated, battered, abandoned. So I was sitting there, looking around, and I asked Grammaw why no one lived there anymore.

"I expect that house is full of snakes, now," she said. Like a lot of people back then, she always hated snakes and feared them.

"So?" I asked. I asked So? a lot. "I don't see why people couldn't live there."

"It's all falling in. There's nothing there but snakes!"

"I don't know," I said. I thought about how everyone always picked on me at home. Yelled at me. Told me what to do. Snakes would be better than almost any human I knew. "I bet I could live over there."

"Well," Grammaw Talbot thought about that for a moment. She said, "I do expect the snakes would keep the rat population down."

Ha-ha, ha. She hadn't forgotten Paul traumatizing Liza and me with that goddamned skewered rat back at Christmas. She wasn't being mean, though. She was actually a very kind old lady who'd had a sad hard time most of her life.

"A family called the Langfords lived there for a long time, it was always the Langford house. You know Hazel Ashcroft?"

"I think so—"

"Hazel's mother was a Langford, one of the last ones. They all died out, and the last ones didn't leave a will, so who knows who really owns it now? I think Hazel probably pays the property tax on it."

"Huh." I always liked hearing about the collapse of families and empires. They were always sad. Even the lost and forgotten Langfords.

"Tell you something else," Grammaw said. "They had that house rented out for a long time, mostly to poor families, and they got poorer and poorer, and nobody took care of the house, and it was a nice house at one time. And then the last family living there was this bottom-poor family, a fat old lady with two half-starved grandchildren running up and down the road in rags."

"What happened to their mom?" I asked.

"Oh, she showed up every now and then," Grammaw said. "Mostly when the relief checks came in. But—that old lady, she'd sit on the porch there in the evenings, and we'd sit out on our porch here, too. And after a while those starving kids would go off to bed, and then just after dark, that old grammaw would lift up her skirts and pee in a coffee can."

"No!" I could imagine it. Ha!

"Yep, she thought no one could see her, but she was wrong."

"And you never told her."

"Of course not." Grammaw Talbot took her glasses off and wiped them, and then put them back on. "And so if you lived over there—well, you'd have to go pee in a coffee can, too."

Well. I probably could if I had to. Maybe.

"But I'll tell you something else," Grammaw said. "Last week, here, I was sleeping there in the big room—" she pointed behind us at the room just off the porch "—and I woke up in the middle of the night and that house was all lit up—it was a-glowing...."

Just then old Pap Talbot came clumping up around the side of the house. He'd been working down in the yard on something and there were grass stains on his pants. He settled back onto the glider.

"You telling her about those lights?" he asked.

"I am," Grammaw said.

Pap Talbot said "Shit." Dragging it out—*Sheeeeeeeeitt.*

"I opened my eyes and that house was all lit up," Grammaw Talbot said again. "Not just like there were lights on inside, the whole house was a-glowing."

Pap Talbot shook his head, slowly. You could tell he was thinking *Sheeeeeeeeitt.*

"I was—scared! I don't know—I didn't know what to think. I thought that old house might be on fire, so I got up and went to the door and looked out and it wasn't on fire, it was just all lit up. Everything was lit up!"

I looked down the road at the old Langford house. It wasn't anything much. Gray-brown, sagging and hunched over, multiflora rose and greenbriers growing all around it, and weeds and young trees and a couple of big trees, all sad in the afternoon sunlight. It was a forgotten house.

I asked, "What'd you do?"

"She went and woke me up," Pap Talbot said.

"I didn't know what else to do," Grammaw Talbot said. "So I woke him up."

"And when I got up here, I didn't see nothing," Pap said. "There wasn't any glow."

"I saw something."

"You were having a dream."

"I saw something," Grammaw Talbot said. "That whole house was a-glowing."

A ghost, I thought.

I asked, "Anybody ever die over there?"

"Oh, hell's fire," Pap Talbot said. One word—*hellsfire*. "There's people died everywhere. There's people died all through this country."

Of course. I knew then it would be a ghost.

I was old enough to already know that Burnt House was full of ghosts. It could be a very scary place, when you thought of all the people that died there, their lost souls glooming around—and I was a kid who thought about things like that a lot. You had only to spend a night or two in Burnt House to start thinking about ghosts— listening to the silence of the night in the winter, water in the creek, a distant car, the crack of ice, and silence, and stillness, or in the summer when the night had millions of voices, frogs and owls and crickets, and lightning bugs that lit up whole hillsides, the night filled with powerful non-human life. Summer or winter, the nights were full of portent—sometimes warm and safe, sometimes icy and scary, and you knew there were ghosts outside, you could feel the presence of the dead if you felt hard enough. Imagination played a part here: I remember reading a knockoff novelization of the film *Night of the Living Dead* and I got up two or three times to make sure the doors and windows were zombie-proof—waking Gran with my checking—and later too being scared reading Stephen King's *The Shining*, and I could easily imagine the giant topiary rabbits hopping around outside with the living night sounds.

Home was a place full of ghosts.

A few years later I was there when Grammaw Talbot died—nearby, at least, in the next room. They sent her home from the hospital that last time and I took turns with Mary Isenhart and my cousin Mark sitting up with her while she passed in and out of consciousness. My Aunt Irene flew in from Minneapolis, full of tears and breakdowns, and she kept hugging everyone and weeping on everyone's shoulders. Grammaw came to at one point and looked at Irene and "Where's Jean?" Jean, my mom. Where was she? I had no idea. In Columbus, a few hours' drive away. But she wasn't in Burnt House. Irene got on the phone and I heard her say, "I don't care what you're doing, Jean—this is it. She's dying. You need to get down here now." And so Mom got in her car and drove down from Columbus for the day—for the afternoon—angry with everyone. Crying, too.

When Mom came down the steps and into the overheated front room she saw me. She asked, "What are you doing here?"

I shrugged. "Helping—"

"You should be up with the Stalnakers," Mom said. "There's nothing you can do to help."

"I am helping," I said.

"It's not good for you to be around people dying."

"Aw, now," Mary Isenhart said. She put an arm around Mom's shoulder. "Your Jackie's a big help to everybody...."

Mary took Mom back to Grammaw Talbot's bedroom. I followed, Irene too. Grammaw woke up and saw Mom standing there and reached out. Mom took her hand and said, "Well, I guess this is goodbye...." Everybody cried and then Mom drove back to Columbus and Grammaw Talbot died early the next morning, still dark, while I was sleeping on the couch in the big room. Mary woke me up and took me to Grammaw Talbot's room.

"I think she's finally passed," Mary said. "She's at peace, now."

I just stood there. I didn't know what to say. Poor Grammaw skinny like a skeleton, dead. Blinds up on the window and nothing but darkness out there.

"She was so sick for so long," Mary said. "Poor thing, you can still smell the cancer a-coming off her."

Now, thousands of miles away and decades later, I know the ghosts in ways different than I did then. There may actually be souls of the dead floating around Burnt

House—certainly enough unhappy people have died there over the years. It wouldn't surprise me. But the ghosts that I think about now are mainly aspects of my memory—my actual memories of those people I knew who are now gone, and the imagined mystery-memories I think those people might have carried with them. These are the ghosts in my life, ghosts that invade my nights, visit my dreams, occupy my time. Every single person I knew in Burnt House is dead now. They're all of them ghosts equally. The Talbots are gone, just like the Langfords, the Isenharts, the Stalnakers. Who remembers any of them except for me? And when I die, no one will remember them, the ghosts.

Dead Don't Care

Of course, you know those people in Burnt House never forgot anything—and they never let you forget that they never forgot, either. Ace Everett knew that—he never forgot it. Ace knew that if you did something wrong or stupid at some point in your life, those people would all remember it forever, and you were going to be publicly bad forever, be a fool forever, you were going to be reminded of your wrongness or your stupidity as long as you lived and then some. All those people, and they were mostly church-goers, too, they all talked about forgiving and forgetting, how Jesus loved the sinners and wanted everyone to forgive trespassers, but Ace didn't think that he had ever met a man or a woman who could be truly honest and say that they forgave or forgot. Nobody in the whole town. Nobody in the county. Nobody. Not any of them. They were all liars and hypocrites and two-faced phonies, and it wasn't right.

Ace knew he was always going to be the boy who was afraid of girls, and he was always going to be the arsonist. Forever. He was afraid of girls. He was an arsonist. Nobody was ever going to forget that. Even after he died, he knew, they'd be talking about him.

Afraid of girls.

House-burner.

Back when he was 12 he and his brothers and a cousin were out on Leading Creek at an old farmhouse his father owned—the farm had once belonged to his grand-uncle or someone, and nobody lived there now, though the house was sturdy enough and dry, if somewhat isolated. Nobody lived there, but the Everetts came out to the farm to cut hay, and maybe stay during deer season, and someone at some point had tacked up on the kitchen wall the November 1966 Playboy centerfold. Right out in the open, next to the rickety dusty table. The girl just hung there on the wall, stretched out on a deer hide with her big round butt staring at everyone.

The boys that day stood around the kitchen gawking at the centerfold. The cousin, Ray Burkehammer, reached out and touched the picture, his finger right on the girl's naked butt, and all the boys hooted.

"Boy, I'd like to grab me a handful of that," Ace's brother, Glenn, said, and they all hooted some more and stood there looking at the girl's butt.

"Yeah," Ace said, after a moment. Then he looked away. "Me too."

"Oh, bullshit." Glenn poked Ace on the shoulder. Glenn, the oldest brother. "You wouldn't know what to do with a girl like that—you wouldn't even look at her."

"He's not even looking at her now," Ray said. He put his finger on the girl again. Tapped the butt. "See this here, Ace? This is an ass!"

"I know it," Ace said. He looked at the centerfold—at the girl. You didn't ever see girls like that around Burnt House. Her butt looked smooth and soft and was pale and framed with tan lines above and below. He looked away again. "Yeah."

"So what would you do if she was here right now?" Ray asked.

"Run away," Glenn said. "He's so scared he wouldn't know what else to do."

"I would not!" Ace said. He looked at the girl again, face down naked on a deer hide. White butt looking at him. "I'd do—something!"

They all laughed.

Glenn asked, "What?"

Ace didn't know. He didn't think. Even later, he couldn't remember thinking about anything, about what he'd really do if there was a naked girl there. Probably he really didn't know what he'd do if there was a naked girl there. That day he just pulled out a pack of matches he was carrying around and he lit one and he held it to the foot of the centerfold.

Ace said, "This is what I'd do."

The boys really hooted, then, and the flaring match caught the glossy paper afire and the naked girl on it went up burning, burning. Ace stepped back, laughing— the girl burning, her legs, that white soft round butt, the deer hide, her brown hair—all burned in a flash.

But the flames didn't stop there, of course—the burning girl flashed up the wall and caught the dangling loose wallpaper afire, and then the ceiling, and then the boys—not hooting now, for sure—they all bolted out into the muddy yard and watched the house burn.

"Man," Ray said, "you really are afraid of that girl."

Ace got a good whipping later, of course. His dad beat him hard, hard, and never forgave him for burning that house down. Nobody forgave him—and nobody forgot it, either, and nobody ever forgot why he burned it down.

Afraid of a picture of a naked girl!

He must be one of those homos.

One of those queers.

He was an arsonist for sure.

House-burner.

Firebug.

Faggot.

Years and years later now and Ace still couldn't go into Butchie's store without people talking about what had happened that day.

"Why, there's ol' Ace—you still afraid of those naked girls, Ace?"

"There's Ace—come to the store to buy himself some matches, I suppose."

"Ace, Ace, he burned down that place."

Ace always tried to act like it didn't matter, but of course it did.

Even Naked Jackson, who was about the only friend Ace had, then, even he never forgot—he'd always tease a little, just like everyone else. Even after all those years. One time Brenda the preacher's wife came over to Naked's to party and she brought along a girlfriend whose name Ace never caught along with the girlfriend's little boy. Brenda the preacher's wife was a fun girl who liked to get away from her husband and drink and smoke pot and snort speed and listen to records—a fun girl, and for a while she would come by Naked's pretty often to hang around. This time they all sat around smoking on the porch of the old house up near the top of Hog Run Naked was renting then, and then Naked and Brenda got up to go inside.

"You're not afraid to stay out here with—" Naked couldn't remember the other girl's name, either. She was just a plain skinny girl with stringy flat brown hair and hollowed-out eyes who kept her mouth shut. "With this one, are you?"

Ace said, "No, I guess not."

And Naked and Brenda went inside and it wasn't but a few minutes before Ace could hear the bedsprings squealing all the way from Naked's bedroom at the back of the house.

Ace and the girlfriend sat and looked at each other for a bit, and then she came over and sat close, thigh touching thigh through jeans, and they necked a little bit, though the girl couldn't really kiss very good because she had a cheek full of snuff and spit—she tasted like soggy wet tobacco—and the girl's little boy just sat there watching them the whole time, staring, staring. That little boy sure had stare-itis. Ace tried to pretend the little boy wasn't there. Felt up the boy's mom a little, some. She was skinny but soft.

When they got up to go inside, the girlfriend said to the boy, "Now, you stay right out here on the porch. Okay?"

The boy nodded. Still had those big giant staring eyes.

"Okay, then." The girl had a lisp, talking through the tobacco and spit.

There was an old bed in the room just in from the porch and Ace and the girlfriend fell onto it, pulling off their clothes, damp in the warm evening.

"Oh—please don't hit me," the girlfriend said. Lisped. Whispered. "Just don't hit me, okay?"

Ace wasn't about to hit her, but he didn't say anything—he thought she was probably one of those sad-like girls that gets hit every now and then, for some reason. He didn't say anything, he just went ahead and screwed her, and then he looked up at one point and saw the girlfriend's little big-eyed boy was up at the window with his hands cupped against the glass. Watching.

"Your boy's been watching us," Ace said when he finished, all sweaty and gasping.

The girlfriend rose up on an elbow and looked at the window. The kid was still there staring in at them. The girlfriend sank back onto the bed.

"It's good for him, I guess," the girlfriend said. "To know about life."

Then Naked and Brenda came back through the house. Naked said, "Look at you two lovebirds! Maybe you're not afraid of girls, after all."

Ace pulled a sheet across his belly. He said, "Aw, Naked. Come on."

A few weeks later Brenda stopped coming around. Her husband, Walter, the preacher, put a stop to that and took her car away. He even called Naked on the phone and told him to leave Brenda alone.

"What the hell is he talking about?" Naked asked Ace. "That Brenda's a grown woman, she can do what she wants! Can't have that sonofabitch calling me like that."

Walter the preacher at one time had liked to hang around the Derrick Lounge in Glenville and drink and smoke pot and have fun like everybody else, but then he found Jesus. Maybe he thought Brenda should find Jesus, too, though so far she hadn't. Naked liked Brenda well enough, and liked her coming around—preachers' wives needed screwing, too, he said—and he didn't like Walter calling him up like that. So one night he decided to get back at Walter by burning his church down—burning it down, or having it burned down.

"What do you say, Ace?" Naked asked. "This is your line of work, right?"

"Aw, man, I don't know."

"You're not afraid, are you? You know that old church'll make a nice fire."

"Well, maybe."

And so a day or two later, in the early hours, Naked pulled his truck up at the Alice Road Baptist Church, in Alice. The church was the last building used in Alice—the others, the old store, the few houses, were all abandoned and half-collapsed piles of aged gray lumber overtaken by thickets of vines and young trees and filth. Across the road from the church there was a swimming hole there where Horn Creek flowed into Leading Creek—pretty good fishing hole, too: when he was a boy, Ace had caught a big pike there once. Biggest fish he ever caught.

The church was on a bank up a little bit from the road, and Naked left his pickup at the bottom of the driveway. They got gallon cans of gasoline from the back of the truck and carried them up and soaked the old church good.

"Light 'er up," Naked said. "You're the expert."

Ace lit a wooden match and tossed it at the church, and

the gasoline caught fire with a whoosh—and whooshed back toward him, too, following a trail of gas that had dribbled from the can. Ace yelled and flung the can at the burning church and the yellow-orange flames caught on the wood and lifted up into the night, wood-smoke and gasoline.

"You did good, pardner!" Naked said.

They started back in the dark toward Burnt House. Ace turned and looked, but once around the first bend in the road, the burning church was out of sight.

"Shit," Ace said. "That was fun."

"I know," Naked said. "You're actually a pretty steady hand, for a scaredy-cat."

•

Ace got up out of bed then and sat in a chair. A little bit of porchlight filtering in through my window on his shoulder, pale. The house I was renting that summer wasn't too far from the railroad tracks, and I could hear a train rumbling. Ace lit a cigarette, his face nice and clean now in the flash of the lighter. Then dark and the burning cigarette and the porchlight through the window.

"You see what I'm saying?" Ace asked. "That shit never stops. Never going to stop, either."

I said, "Go somewhere else, then."

"There isn't anywhere else," Ace said. "You know that as much as anybody."

In the dark I saw his head move—a nod.

"Yeah, I know," I said. But I knew that differently than he did. But, yeah. For Ace—clean now, more or less sober now, married, with a good job driving a well-service truck for Haliburton—for Ace, I guess there wasn't any place else to go. Burnt House was the world. Lewis County. Gilmer County. This was where he was going to spend his life. Where he was going to die.

After some silence I said, "Ace, I'm sorry."

"It's not your fault." Ace stubbed out the cigarette and climbed back into bed. "It's sure everybody else's fault, though. Everybody in that town."

He put his hand against my face.

"Well, Ace, just don't hit me," I said. Teasing. Smiling in the dark. Trying to make a joke. The wrong thing to do—but people do wrong things, sometimes, without thinking. Hurting people sometimes comes a lot easier than thinking.

Ace was silent. I could hear him breathing, feel his breath. He pulled his hand away from my face.

"You know I'd never hit a girl," Ace said after a while. "I never even liked hitting men—I don't like fighting. It's stupid."

"Yeah?" I asked.

"Some men do." Ace rolled away onto his back. Took a deep breath, exhaled. Shook his head. "Aw, Jesus."

Sounded—sad. Was he crying?

"Ace?" I asked. I put my hand on his chest—smooth, warm. "What's wrong?"

"I'll tell you," Ace said. "I'll tell you—see, there was this one time I killed a boy."

•

It was that Mark Sitton who came up with the idea of robbing graves, though he never knew it. He was down at Butchie's buying beer one time, and he was telling everybody hanging around the store how he'd taken his granddad up to visit an old cemetery, and then he found an old arm bone some groundhog had dug up.

"That's that Catholic cemetery way back on that hill," old Gid Ellyson said.

"Right," Mark said. "And—"

"That's a hard place to get to."

"Yeah," Mark said. "And—"

"Course, if you're dead, you don't really care if it's hard to get to or not."

"No," Mark said. "But—"

"Though I expect nobody really wants to go up there at all, dead or no."

"But—" Mark said. Took a breath. "But those graves were all about a hundred years old, and I swear that arm looked brand-new."

Ace wondered how Mark might know what a new-looking arm-bone might look like and how it was different from an old-looking arm-bone. Mark was just another big-talking liar.

"Well, a groundhog'll dig up about anything," Gid said. "I suppose."

"I thought about taking that arm home," Mark said. "But I just put it back down the hole."

"Groundhog don't need an old bone."

Ace was sitting back in the corner, just listening. And it came to him clear. An idea. Like a flash. A revelation. Somebody could go out there and rob the goddamn dead! Now, that city-boy Mark was a fool, he didn't even see the idea he had. What if that arm had a hand on it that had a ring on it? Would you just toss it back down the hole for the groundhogs to toss back out again? And what about all the other arms just buried down there with jewels on them? And all the necks with jewels.

Nobody had ever thought of that, had they?

So. That first cemetery he robbed was up off of Laurel Run. He parked down the road a bit, then slogged back up the creek in the water over slippery rocks, falling a couple of times, all wet and tired by the time he got to the graves. It was just on the other side of the creek from the road, and that's what worried him—not ghosts but someone coming down the road at night, not minding their own business, and seeing something out there in the graveyard, seeing a blink of Ace's s flashlight or hearing the thud of his mattock digging in the earth. Somebody nosy like that could call the law, or they might just want to investigate on their own. That would be a problem. It would be better if people thought he was a ghost and took off running.

But if anybody saw anything, nothing happened. The

digging went quickly, loose-like soil with small gravel. One newer grave had a vault, which he didn't take the time to bust open, but the others, maybe they were older graves or poorer ones, he didn't bother looking at the stones, were just dirt down to the box, metal or rotted wood, and he was able to pry those open pretty easily. The people were all wet and molded and rotted in the boxes—these graves were close to the water table, and Laurel Run often flooded, it was a stupid place for a graveyard. Each time he opened a casket, Ace felt excitement build up like the day before Christmas or a birthday, like something good you knew was going to happen—but, then, well, hell. In the end it really *was* just like Christmas or a birthday—you didn't ever get anything good. Just some shit you didn't want. Here you got just a wet box with a moldy old corpse in it. Just bones, mostly, with a bunch of muddy clay and silt that had washed in. Nothing much, really. Nothing to be scared of. One of the skulls came apart when he was prying at it, but two others came out nearly whole though with moldy hanks of hair hanging from them, and he found two wedding rings and seven buttons. A handful of good loose teeth.

Ace didn't think anything of the people. They were just dead.

A few days later, Ace took his loot over by Naked Jackson's. Ace had no idea what to do with it. What should you do with an old wedding ring? Melt it down? Sell it as an antique?

"Give it to a girl?" Naked asked. "If you're not too scared."

"Aw, man," Ace said.

"You sure? Give that ring to a nice girl?"

"Aw, Naked."

"It's nothing to be ashamed of, liking a girl."

"Naked—"

"Oh, I know," Naked said. He cackled a little, high. "I'm just giving you shit."

"I know it," Ace said. "But, Naked—I'm tired of taking shit. You know?"

Naked knew a guy in Pittsburgh. A few days later he was back. The friend in Pittsburgh would pay for the rings melted down at the daily rate for gold, a couple of dollars apiece for the buttons, maybe three apiece for the better teeth—there was always a demand for human molars, for cufflinks and tie-tacks—and maybe $100 each for the skulls, depending on condition. You could always get good money for skulls.

So then for a little while Ace made his living robbing graves. There were so many old forgotten cemeteries scattered through the hills, out in the woods, all of them full of dead people who didn't need whatever it was they were carrying with them. Ace for sure wasn't afraid of the dead, like some folks might be. The dead were the least of his worries, ever. They were like rocks in the ground, dissolving bones in dissolving boxes—though he did think about them as people, sometimes, on late quiet nights when he'd bang his heavy mattock down deep into the stony earth, and he would think about who the dead people were in the graves, the people he was robbing— he wondered about them, but he wasn't scared of them. They were poor dead people, of course, mostly, old and poor and forgotten—nobody ever put flowers out there on those graves, or decorated the tombstones, the people were just rotting alone, with no family. Ace wondered about them, a little, wondered if they'd been good or bad or if they'd ever done anything while they were alive, but he wasn't afraid of them. Ghosts weren't a problem.

"You're making some pretty good hauls, there," Naked said.

They were sitting in Ace's trailer passing a bowl back and forth. Ace had robbed three cemeteries in one week, and was tired out.

"I'll tell you, man," Ace said. "It's a lot of work, digging those graves."

"Hell, yes, it's a lot of work!" Naked said. He slouched down on the couch and rubbed at his flat belly. "You might as well get yourself a job at the Go-Mart, get paid by the hour."

"What? Go-Mart wouldn't give me a j—" Ace began, but stopped. Naked was making a joke. Everybody knew Ace had been picked up four or five times for shoplifting at Go-Mart.

"What you need is an assistant," Naked said.

Ace thought about that. He said, "But then I'd only make half as much."

"But you'd dig up twice as much," Naked said. "Maybe three times as much. And who says you have to share even? Go sixty-forty with 'em."

"Hell." Ace smoked a bit, and thought. Those dead people had all mostly been poor in life but they carried things to the grave, things they didn't need, and there were probably enough rings and brooches and buttons and gold teeth—and bones and molars and skulls—to make a helper worth the trouble. Ace said, "More like seventy-thirty."

After thinking about it for a few more days, Ace decided that Jimmy Joliff was his man—his boy, his helper, his assistant. Jimmy lived with his parents down below Glenville, on Sinking Creek, but he showed up in Burnt House every now and then, buying dope from Naked to resell to his neighbors. A quiet-like boy with pale eyes, he never said much. All Ace knew was that Jimmy had dropped out of school, spent a couple of months in the reformatory for animal cruelty and petty larceny, and that he looked like he was capable of swinging a mattock in the middle of the night. Ace mainly thought about Jimmy's broad back—the boy had a hole-digging back for sure.

The night they went out to rob graves, Ace didn't want Jimmy's parents to think anything, to see him go out and maybe ask questions, so he parked down the road in a turnout under some trees by the river a half-mile or so from Jimmy's place and waited in his car, and Jimmy was late, of course. Half-hour, forty-five minutes, an hour. What the hell? Ace was still waiting when the sheriff's patrol car went by, and slowed, and stopped. Then the car reversed and slid into the turnout, just in front of Ace's car. Deputy Doy Caldwell got out of the car and walked back.

"What're you doing out here?" Doy asked.

"Me? Nothing." Ace said. Which was the truth—he was just waiting, sitting, not even smoking dope—and it was a simple truth, too. Always paid to keep it simple talking to the law.

"Nothing, huh?" Doy asked. He bent over and looked in the back seat. "And here I always heard you were a hard worker."

"Me? Aw, hell no."

"No?" Doy straightened up. A car came around the bend, slowed as its driver saw Doy there talking, but then headed on down toward Grantsville. "Everybody's wrong, then, huh? You're really just a big loafer?"

"Man, I guess." Ace thought, What the hell? Go bother somebody else. He said, "I'm just sitting here in the car taking it easy."

"Some people are lazy, and some people are crazy," Doy said. "I guess you're one of the lazy ones, huh?"

"I expect I am," Ace said.

"Well, I guess you're an honest man, too," Doy said. "You won't even lie about being lazy."

"Oh, I was raised to tell the truth," Ace said.

"Yeah?" Doy took a step back. "Well, you just keep telling the truth, then. Have a good night."

Doy turned and walked away.

Ace lit a cigarette. It was a bad sign, Doy stopping like that. But maybe he was just screwing with me. He was probably just screwing with me. Of course he was screwing with me. He didn't have anything better to do. Goddamn law. Ace watched Doy get in his car and drive off—and the son of a bitch pulled out onto the road without even using his turn signal. All these people in this country were just a bunch of goddamn hypocrites.

Ace sat and waited. A car went by, then a pickup. Jimmy was taking his goddamn time. Two more cars. A squirrel dropped down from a tree and scooted across the road and down the bank towards the Little Kanawha. Then Jimmy came around the bend, walking with a hitch in his step, hand in his pocket, taking his time. Hand in his pocket like he was playing with his pecker. Like he didn't care about anything. He just walked on up and got in the car, no hurry.

"Where're you been?" Ace asked. "You about ruined everything."

"I'm not late, am I?" Jimmy asked. Liar. He knew he was late.

"This is work," Ace said. "You have to pay attention. You have to be on time."

"Oh, I'm not that late."

After his third grave-robbing, word started getting around, people noticed the dug-up graves, and the paper ran a little piece about vandals hitting the old cemeteries. Ace moved his work off a bit, to Richie County, Wood County. But after four months the heat died down, or Ace thought it had until that deputy stopped and talked to him along the road—and, well, that still probably didn't mean anything, and Ace decided he wasn't going to think about it. The law just screwed with people. And then people just screwed with each other, nothing was good, hypocrites everywhere, everybody in the whole world just a damn liar—

•

I said, "It's okay, Ace. It was a long time ago."

"Yeah."

"It's okay, really."

"You know, you can't tell anybody about this," Ace

said. "You can't."

"I won't."

"Please."

"No," I said. "I won't."

"Not unless something happens to me," Ace said. "If something happens to me—well, I won't care, then."

"I won't tell," I said.

Something happens to everyone, eventually.

•

Anyway, with Jimmy not knowing anything about the job, it was probably easiest to stay closer to home. Gilmer County, Lewis County. There was a cemetery on Richbottom Run that was isolated and old, they hadn't buried anyone there in 20 or 25 years, so it might be a pretty good score. Of course, you couldn't just park in front of some graveyard and start digging, you always had to go in the back way, somehow, and for Richbottom Run that meant cutting over on Lower Big Run and hiding the car somewhere and then hiking back over the hill in the dark. It was a lot of work, but if it paid off, it paid off. Ace had done it enough times that it didn't seem to be that big of a deal. Just a job of hard work. Naked Jackson thought he was crazy, working so hard in the middle of the night like that. But Naked was—lazy, not crazy. He was just lazy. All Naked wanted to do was sell dope and play pool and beat people up every now and then. Basically, just sit around all day. Naked sure made good money selling dope, but he sure had more risk, too. The law didn't like dope dealers unless the dope dealers were paying them off, and Naked was too tight with his money to bribe the lawmen. He was just taking his chances. So maybe he was lazy and crazy both.

"What about you?" Ace asked Jimmy. They were driving in the dark, making a big circle around the back of the county. "Are you lazy or crazy?"

"Aw, hell," Jimmy said. "I don't know. That's a tough one."

"You're either one or the other," Ace said.

"Crazy, I guess," Jimmy said. "That lady said I was disturbed when I was at the youth camp."

"Oh," Ace said. "Yeah." That. Shouldn't even have asked about that—Ace liked cats and dogs, he didn't want to hear about any of that, about how Jimmy had been picked up and sent off for animal cruelty—for cat torturing. For stealing people's cats and crucifying them, nailing them alive to the trunks of trees and the walls of old buildings and leaving them there to die. For tying them up and dragging them behind his dad's car until they were just fluffs of bloody hair. His parents knew all about it and didn't even try to stop him—the law found a half-dozen cats nailed up to the walls of their barn. Jimmy was crazy all right.

"Well," Ace said. Crazy or disturbed or whatever he was, Jimmy did have that hole-digging back. "So, what're you going to do with all that money we make tonight?"

"Oh, I don't know," Jimmy said. "I guess I was thinking about getting a new deer rifle."

"Well, that's something."

Jimmy was about half-stupid, too.

They came down Hog Run and into Burnt House and turned at Page's store, and went past the post office, and Jimmy said he had to take a leak.

"You can go when we get there," Ace said. "Won't be that long."

"C'mon, Ace. I can't wait."

Well, hell, Ace thought. Little whiner. Piss his pants for all I care. Except he'd probably piss on the car seat, too. Well, hell. Jimmy pulled over across the road from Butchie's store, in front of the schoolhouse and stopped the car in the shadows.

"Don't take all night," Ace said.

Jimmy got out of the car and crossed the road to the store. Ace thought about going in, too, but there'd be people in there to talk to, people he didn't want to talk to, and this was work, and he decided to stay in the car, in the shadows. Still, he wasn't hidden. There were a couple of old-timers sitting on a bench there in front of the door—Gid Ellyson and Simon Moyer—and they were staring at him. Finally, old Gid got up and hobbled over to the car.

"Where're you boys off to tonight?" he asked.

"Going fishing," Ace said.

"Good time of the year for that," Gid said.

Gid stood there looking the car over, looking Ace over—Ace was reminded of that lawman, except Gid didn't mean any real harm. Just looking around, being nosy.

"I used to go fishing," Gid said.

I suppose you used to do a lot of things, Ace thought. But all you do now is talk.

"There used to be fish in these rivers, then."

"I suppose," Ace said. Damn talking old man.

"Once I caught me a 42-inch pike," Gid said. "Biggest fish I ever caught. He was a—a giant. Hell, yes. Down there on the Little Kanawha. I didn't even know what to do with him."

"Yeah...." Ace kept watching Butchie's door.

"Ate him."

"Yeah?"

"But there's no fishing around here anymore," Gid said. "All those oil spills, all that dirt in the river. Those fish're about all killed off."

"Yeah," Ace said.

"You boys'll just be wasting your time."

"Well...." Ace was starting to get irritated. Gid should just—shut up.

"Unless you boys are gong be doing a little drinking, too." Gid cackled, his toothless mouth gaping. "Or smoking some of that weed you boys smoke, huh?"

"What?" Ace looked from the doorway to the old man's ugly gaping face. "Oh—hell, no!"

The old man just cackled.

Jimmy came out of the store carrying a 16-ounce can of Stroh's.

"Hey," the old man said. "Your little boyfriend's got the right idea, there—but he only got the one can of beer. That won't be enough."

Jimmy came around and got in the car, the beer almost spilling.

Ace asked, "You didn't get me anything?"

"Oh—you didn't ask." Jimmy held out the can. "Want a sip?"

"I'm not drinking your spit!"

Old Gid stumbled around the car and now he leaned in Jimmy's window. "So, you boys're going fishing, huh?"

"What?" Jimmy asked.

"I think we'll go up there around Burnsville, below the dam," Ace said.

"We are?" Jimmy asked.

Gid leaned into the car even more, like he was going to kiss Jimmy, but he was just looking around the car. Nosy. Gid asked, "Where's your fish poles?"

"In the trunk," Ace said. He put the car in gear. "Well, we got to go."

"Well, good luck to you," Gid said. He straightened up as much as he could straighten and stepped away from the car and nodded.

Ace pulled back onto the road and drove out of Burnt House. To get to Big Run, he took a long way, circling around in case anybody—that talking Gid Ellyson, maybe—was watching where they went, went over a hill and down Route 33 toward Glenville, then up Alice Road to Alice. Alice was always a good memory. Burning down that church was fun. Reverend Walter, though, was putting up a new church right were the old one had been— not a new wooden building but some sort of doublewide trailer painted white. Ace wondered if Brenda ever got her freedom. If Walter ever learned his lesson. He must have. Naked hadn't said anything about him in a while.

"We're going back to Burnt House?" Jimmy asked.

Ace said, "No."

He turned at the church and crossed Leading Creek on a rusting iron bridge right above the swimming hole and went down a graveled road that led past the old Everett farm, where Ace had set the centerfold on fire. Now Ace had a bad memory to chase the good memory of the church. Ace braced himself in the car, waited for half-stupid crazy Jimmy to say something.

"Hey," Jimmy said. Of course. "That's where your granddad's old farm was, wasn't it?"

Nobody ever forgot that fire. Nobody ever would. Jimmy had grown up clear on the other side of the county and he was just a baby when it happened, and here he knew all about it, or thought he did. All those gossips, all those people talking too much.

Now, though, in the car, on his way to rob some graves, all Ace said was, "It wasn't my Pap's farm—it was his brother's."

Ace could feel Jimmy sitting there next to him—knew Jimmy was probably smiling—he was just a half-stupid kid who hadn't even finished high school, he was a goddamn cat-torturer, and he thought this was funny.

"Yeah," Jimmy said. "They say you burned down that house just because you were afraid of the naked girl."

"They say that, huh? Who's they?"

"Oh, everybody." Jimmy was laughing. "Man, I wouldn't be afraid of any naked girl!"

"Bullshit," Ace said.

"I'd stick it right in her!"

"You would not," Ace said. "You wouldn't know what to do with a naked girl."

"Huh—well, at least I wouldn't be afraid of one!" Jimmy was laughing his stupid laugh. "At least I wouldn't burn down the damn house just because I saw one!"

Ace hit the brakes and the car skidded on the gravel and came to a stop. Jimmy lost hold of his beer and it tumbled to the floor and the car was silent.

"How'd you like to get your goddamn teeth slapped out?" Ace asked. "I mean it."

Jimmy didn't say anything. The car smelled like beer.

"Goddamn it, I asked you a question. You want to get the shit kicked out of you right now?"

Jimmy said, "Aw, Ace, come on. You know I didn't mean anything."

"Hell you didn't," Ace said. "You meant the same thing as everybody else in this goddamn country."

Ace stared at Jimmy, at his shadowy shape, but Jimmy looked straight ahead, shaking his head a little. He didn't say anything, which might have saved his life right then, for a little bit. After some more silence, Ace took his foot off the brake and the car crept forward into the dark.

Jimmy said, "Man, you need to learn how to take a goddamn joke."

"Shut up, you little shit."

Ace drove on, mostly uphill through the trees, until the road—by now pretty much a track—dipped back into a holler. Ace pulled the car off as much as he could and then turned it off. Night forest sounds flooded through the open windows.

"You about ready to grow up and stop being an asshole?" Ace asked.

"I'm not the asshole around here," Jimmy said.

Jimmy sounded testy but to hell with him. Ace got out of the car and went around and opened the trunk. Jimmy got out and came around too. Ace handed Jimmy a spade and a burlap bag.

"We should be able to find it," Ace said. All they had to do was go up the hill in the dark and back down the other side, and the graveyard should be right around there somewhere.

"*Should* find it?'" Jimmy asked. "Man, we better do better than that."

"Well, shit on you," Ace said. He took a mattock from

the trunk and a burlap bag of his own, and he shut the trunk softly. No noise.

"Don't you ever talk to me like that," Jimmy said. "I'm an adult."

Ace laughed, standing there in the dark. "Yeah, I'll talk to you like an adult when you act like one," he said. "Let's go."

They climbed noisily up the hill in the dark. Noisily—that wasn't the word, they made a goddamn racket—enough to wake the dead, Ace thought. Ha. Dried-up leaves, busted tree limbs, stones kicked loose rolling down the hill. Every time he climbed a hill in the dark, Ace figured someone could hear them climb a mile or two away, but nobody ever did, or if they did, nobody ever said anything. Still, it was damn noisy. How did the Indians do it? Everybody always said they moved so quiet through the woods back in the old days. Ace always heard that. But after climbing a dozen or so hills through the dark woods, after a near-lifetime of squirrel hunting and deer hunting, Ace decided that it was all a bunch of shit, that Indians must have made noise, too, every goddamn thing moving through the woods made noise. Ever hear a damn little chipmunk digging through the leaves looking for a nut? What about a fox? Ever hear a big deer? They all made a hell of a noise. Dumb bastards. To hell with the Indians. It was fine to make noise.

Maybe half-way up the holler, Ace came to a wide-seeming place—in the dark, it seemed wide—water dripping over slick slate. The air felt cooler by the rocks, and Ace stopped to catch his breath, and then he thought, To hell with it, and he sat down to rest on the soft damp mossy bank.

Jimmy was lagging behind. Struggling noisily up the hill, up the holler. Ace heard him fall, crashing into the leaves—then flail around and fall again. But he got up and kept coming, and he passed by Ace, still heading up. Maybe he didn't see Ace sitting there in the dark. Maybe he saw him and didn't care.

"Go ahead and take a break," Ace said.

Jimmy didn't stop. He said, "To hell with this shit."

Sounded mad. Ace thought. Hell with him—what does he have to be mad about? He's getting his 25 percent. Little goddamn whiner.

Jimmy mumbled something more.

Ace asked, "What?"

Jimmy stopped a few feet above Ace standing on the damp slate. "I said, to hell with this goddamn shit."

"Aw, shut up," Ace said.

"To hell with you, too," Jimmy said. "Got me out here in the middle of the night doing shit I wouldn't be doing in the daytime, either. Fuck you."

"Fuck you, too," Ace said. "Head back if this is so hard, you little girl."

"If I was a little girl, you'd be a-scared of me," Jimmy said. "You know if I was a little girl, I'd kick your ass."

Ace took his heavy mattock and poked it out quickly in the dark, not even a swing, not enough space or maybe even time to swing it—he poked it out quick and hit the heavy flat head of the mattock right in the side of Jimmy's knee. He never really knew why he did it, never really thought about it too much afterwards, tried hard not to think about it, he didn't really want to ever think about it, ever, it just happened, just like he burned the centerfold, it just happened, he was just fed up and tired of taking shit and he poked the head of the mattock hard into Jimmy's dark shape there in the holler and hit him in the knee and knocked him down and Jimmy squawked and was thrashing around. Then Ace was quick up on his feet and he swung the mattock up for power and then swung it down like he was cutting into a stump and he dug it into Jimmy's shoulder.

Jimmy screamed.

"Just shut up," Ace said.

Jimmy slid down the wet slate and into some leaves.

He was still thrashing around. Ace heard him gasp, then say, "Aw, fuck!"

"Just shut up," Ace said.

"No, Ace!"

Ace slipped and landed on Jimmy in the dark. Jimmy was pushing up with one arm, trying to push Ace away. Ace knocked Jimmy's hand away and poked him hard with the mattock handle and Jimmy gasped, and Ace swung the mattock down on Jimmy again and he screamed. Then again, and Jimmy yelled, "Don't kill me, Ace!"

Message For You

One day I stopped by Page's store to get some gas, and Page's wife, Maud, came out to fill my tank. We were talking about something or other when someone over across the road at the post office started screaming.

"What's that?" I asked.

Maud didn't know. Somebody sure was screaming, though. Then we saw a woman run around the side of the post office and back behind Bess's garage.

"Holy Jesus!" Maud said, and she darted inside the store to get Page.

I just stood there for a moment, and then I started walking toward the post office. Bess came out from the office, and three or four other people, and they gathered around in a loose semi-circle. About the time I got there, Bess's husband, Doc, came out of the garage carrying a hoe. I realized—Oh, a snake.

And, yes, a big blacksnake was coiled around base of the post office flagpole.

"He's a big one," someone said.

"He's not doing any harm," Bess said.

I heard a shout, and looked up to see Page running across the road carrying a shotgun. But Doc Wiant just came up with the hoe and hacked the snake's head off.

"Aw, he wasn't doing any harm," Bess said. "He's just an old blacksnake."

Doc said, "Don't like snakes around the house."

Bess said, "You'd rather have rats?"

Page was disappointed he got there too late with the shotgun. "Well," he said, "I would've shot that snake."

Everybody nodded. Yeah, he probably would have shot that snake. So there.

At that point the young woman who'd been screaming came back around the garage, and she looked sort of familiar. She looked at me like she thought I was familiar, too. But then she looked at the snake, and she shuddered.

"Oh, God," she said, "I hate snakes."

Yeah, we could all see that. She sure hated snakes. We nodded.

Bess helped the young woman gather up mail she'd dropped—a government check, it looked like, and maybe a gas bill, and another envelope or two. No one really said too much to her, or even looked at her, as if she made everyone nervous and uncomfortable. No—no as if, she really *did* make everyone nervous and uncomfortable. After a bit she got in her rusty beat-up Chevy and headed down the road.

I walked back to the store with Page and he was all excited about the snake—everyone in Burnt House got excited about snakes.

"Why, just last week I killed a copperhead out in back of the house that was big around as my arm!"

I nodded. I bet he did. So there.

Inside the store, Maud was behind the counter and old Gid Ellyson was sitting on the bench under the bear head. Page put the shotgun up and told everyone how Doc chopped the head off the snake.

"Snakes are thick this year," old Gid said.

"Hell, snakes are thick like this every year!" Page said. "These hills are a-crawling with snakes!"

"That's what everybody says," I said. I leaned

back against the door frame. "I was on the hill once picking blackberries and I looked down and there was a copperhead crawling right across my foot."

I nodded. Most all snake stories you hear are bullshit, but mine was true. I stood stock-still and watched the snake—a really quite beautiful mottled brown-bronze and gray—cross my foot and disappear under some leaves and rocks. I didn't feel anything where it touched my foot, felt only the slight sharp scrape of the blackberry thorns against my bare arms. That day I stood there in Page's store and I nodded again. So there.

"Oh, that's happened to me many times," Page said. He upped me. Dismissed me. So there! "Once when I was your age I stepped into a whole nest of copperheads—you bet I did some high stepping getting out of there!"

Maud said, "Growing up in Webster County, we never saw a copperhead. Just rattlesnakes—those big timber rattlers."

"And you never see a rattlesnake in Gilmer County," Page said. So there. Nobody could get up on Page.

Old Gid Ellyson had been listening attentively, or pretending to listen attentively—he was pretty much deaf by that time.

"Well, now," he said finally. "You know, a hog'll eat a snake."

He didn't bother nodding, so I nodded for him. No doubt a hog would eat a snake. So there. I paid for my gas and started to leave.

"Now, you know who that screaming girl was, don't you?" Page asked.

I waited. He wouldn't have asked if he wasn't going to tell me.

Page lowered his voice. "That's that Ratliff girl who killed her sister."

I said, "Oh!"

"Electrocuted her." Page nodded.

I knew the girl. Janice Ratliff. Four or five years older

than me. Her grandmother went to church with Gran and would stop by the house sometimes, and Mrs. Ratliff would bring Janice along, an obnoxious, pudgy, troll-like girl with hollowed eyes and stringy brown hair. Nobody ever talked to her, everybody just looked away when she was around, even her grandmother. She was bad luck—a jinx. What happened was that one time, years before, she was taking a bath with her little sister and somehow pulled a radio—a radio!—into the tub. "Mammaw, this water's a-biting me," she was supposed to have yelled, or at least that's what Mrs. Ratliff told Gran she yelled. This water's a-biting me. The little sister died. Janice lived and became a grim little girl, annoying and weird, and I couldn't stand her, and one time Mrs. Ratliff and Janice were over and Janice just sat there in a hard straight-backed chair glowering at me with her mouth pursed shut, pouty, disturbing my reading, until I finally I said, "You fucking creep—why don't you take my radio and go play in the creek?" Which was harsh, even for an asocial teen like I was. Harsh, but Janice Ratliff was a horrible child, a horrible young woman. And here she'd grown up to be a nervous, skinny adult who was afraid of snakes and caused big scenes and made people uncomfortable.

"That girl is all kinds of bad business," Page said.

"I always heard she killed that sister on purpose," Maud said.

"No way," I said. She was creepy and unpleasant but even I didn't believe that.

"Yes!" Page said. He was getting all worked up again. "Who all keeps a radio in the bathroom?"

"She was maybe like seven years old when that happened," I said.

"Well," Maud said. "You know, lots of those bad ones start out young."

Gid Ellyson followed me out to my car and stood looking over at the post office, and down the road. It was quiet out now and Doc Wiant was out mowing his grass—

he had a riding lawnmower, a rarity in that country then.

"Yeah, those snakes can be a threat," Gid said.

"That's true, I guess." I opened my car door to get in.

"Don't forget, now," Gid said. "The world's got a message for you."

"Yeah?" I asked. I'd heard Gid say that before a time or two but I never knew what he meant. A message. This time I asked, "What's the message?"

"Oh, you'll know it when you hear it." Gid cackled and walked away down the road.

"Right," I said. I got in the car and drove off. Back then I thought Gid was crazy.

About two hours later I was over in Glenville and I ran into Janice Ratliff coming out of the bank. She saw me, too, and recognized me. She hesitated, like she wanted to talk to me.

"Well, looks like you're doing good these days," I said.

Janice cocked her head and looked at me, like she knew I was lying. She looked bad. It was hard to believe she was only 25 or so. She was all skinny now, but her hair was still stringy, and her eyes were big and brown and had circles under them, and her teeth were snaggly and snarly and stained brown from tobacco, and she just seemed deeply creepy and unhappy. Maybe she did kill that sister on purpose.

"You know," Janice finally said. "You was never very nice to me when you was little."

I said, "Oh...."

"Even now you're all stuck-up," Janice said. "Think you're so smart and you're really just kind of a whore."

And then she walked off.

So there.

Custom Deluxe

Then there was the night when they all decided that they ought to hunt some bats. Shoot the bats with shotguns when they scrambled out that hole up by the roof of Debbie Renser's house. Once the bats came out the hole they were hard to hit, fluttering off into the dark, and there was only a second, less than a second, to pull the trigger and shoot the sons of bitches. By the time it was full dark, of course, no one could really see the bats any more, everyone was just guessing where the bats were, so they all just took turns more or less firing the shotgun up into the night sky and shooting the corner off Debbie's house.

Nobody really wanted to shoot the house but they were all drunk and high and careless, and it got shot up anyway. Debbie was in the kitchen the whole time—everybody could see her messing around in there, trying to feed the baby—and every now and then she stuck her head out the back door and yell at them to stop.

"I want you dumb sons of bitches to stop shooting my goddamn house!"

Everybody laughed at her, of course. People would nudge Kenny Joiner, who was living with Debbie, and laugh at him, too. He was in for it later. He wasn't going to get any that night, nope. Poor Kenny.

At some point Naked Jackson went over and sat on the grass next to Liza. He asked, "You want to go to town?"

There wasn't much shooting left to do. Nobody could see any bats, and Kenny was running low on shells.

"Well." Liza sat back in the dark. "Sure, I guess...."

"If you don't want to—"

"No—"

"To hell with you, then," Naked said.

Liza jumped up and headed around the corner of the house, crying or something.

Naked thought, Damn girl.

But when Naked got to his feet and wandered down the hill to his truck, Liza was waiting for him there, standing in the shadows.

"Change your mind?" Naked asked.

"Never had to change it," Liza said. "You know that."

Back up the hill behind the house people were talking. Someone had started a fire, and Naked could see people were moving around the flames. Dancing or whatever.

"I'm not taking you straight home," Naked said.

"That's fine."

Crazy girl. Naked got in the truck and Liza went around and got in the other side. But when Naked turned the key, nothing happened. The battery was almost new, a Die-Hard he'd had someone steal for him from Page Westfall's truck in Burnt House, and the engine was grinding but wouldn't catch.

"What's wrong?" Liza asked.

"Hell." Naked smacked the steering wheel. "That damn son of a bitch!"

"It's not starting?" Liza asked.

"No shit, it's not starting," Naked said. He got out and popped the hood but he couldn't see anything in the dark. Dark down there in the engine, and busted. Goddamn piece of shit. Liza got out of the truck and was standing there, too.

"Go see if somebody's got a flashlight," Naked said.

In a few minutes there was a crowd of helpful, drunk, high men standing around the dead Ford. Kenny had a flashlight. Made more shadows than light. Couldn't see a damn thing.

"Try it again," somebody said.

Naked, in the truck, turned the key. Grinding.

"Okay, stop."

Liza and a couple of other girls were watching standing back.

"Fuel pump," someone said.

"It got gas?"

"If you want, I'll give you a jump."

"It's the alternator."

"No—goddamn fuel pump!"

"Fuck it," Naked said. The hell. He got out of the truck and stood next to the open hood. Everybody was staring down at the engine. "Piece of shit."

Naked kicked the fender. The men scrambled back.

"The hell with it," Naked said. "I'll get me a new one."

"If it's just the fuel pump...."

"Hell with the fuel pump!"

"Lot of money...."

"Fuel pump's cheaper than whole a new truck...."

"I'm still saying it's the damn alternator!"

"If I need a new goddamn truck," Naked said, "I'm gonna get me a new goddamn truck."

Everyone stood around in the dark, nodding.

Naked nodded too.

"You can fix it tomorrow," Liza said. "We can maybe get a tow...."

"Park it and fuck it," Naked said. He didn't care, too much—the truck wasn't really his, anyway, it wasn't in his name, it actually belonged to some girl over in Sutton who owed him a bunch of money on a speed deal so he took her truck and he'd just been driving it for a few months and the girl was too scared to do anything about it. He never had the title in his name—or registration, or insurance. It was easy to walk away from. "Debbie can have it, if she wants it."

After a while everyone drifted back up to Debbie's house to sit around and drink and smoke some more. Sometime well after midnight Kenny Joiner gave them a ride back as far as Burnt House, to Liza's mom's house. He dropped them off down at the end of the yard, and then scooted back to see if he could make things right with Debbie.

Liza wouldn't let Naked come inside and sleep, made him sleep outside on the porch glider. Naked didn't argue much, just thought, Damn girl, and settled back to sleep in the cool night air.

He woke to see Liza's mom, Dorothy, sitting there drinking her coffee.

"Well, well, well." Dorothy looked at him over the top of her cup. Like she was hiding behind the cup.

"It's morning, huh?" Naked rolled to his side and looked around. Yeah, it was morning. A nice morning, dew sparkling on grass. Some white-faced cows in the pasture across the creek.

"I guess you walked here," Dorothy said.

"Oh, my truck broke down. We got a ride."

"Liza's still in there asleep," Dorothy said. "Go get yourself come coffee."

"I need to get a new truck today," Naked said. He sat up and stretched.

"I swear," Dorothy said. "You never do wear a shirt, do you?"

Liza got up after awhile and made a show of fussing over him—cooking breakfast, even—while Dorothy sat there watching, all frowns, not even making a show of approving. She was an honest old bitch, at least. She hated Naked so much she even let Liza take her car to get him off the property.

"Thank you, Mrs. Stalnaker," Naked said. He smiled

as sweetly as he could—maybe a little too sweet. Dorothy didn't say anything and went back inside the house.

"Remember, I'm the one that made you breakfast," Liza said. "I'm the one that's giving you a ride."

"Aw, don't be jealous," Naked said. He was happy in the mornings—the air felt good, and the sun was shining. Naked was renting a house in Glenville, then, so Liza drove Dorothy's car down Horn Creek, and then through Alice to Glenville, so Naked could get some cash from the hiding place in his house. Then up to Pricetown, just this side of Weston, to see Gerald, Liza's brother, who managed a used car lot.

They walked down the lot past the cars to where the pickups were parked. There were two Fords and three Chevys, and one of the Chevys was pretty nice, and the right price, a red 1975 Custom Deluxe, not as nice a truck as the Cheyenne or the Silverado, but a good solid work truck. Naked got up and sat in it—the interior was in good shape. He looked at the odometer. Just over 92,000 miles.

"Shit," Naked said. "Who's been driving this?"

"Guy who owned it before drove it to Alaska and back," Gerald said. "That's what he said, at least."

"Who from around here would drive all the way to Alaska?" Naked asked. "And back."

Gerald shrugged. "Guy who owned this truck, I guess."

"Shit," Naked said. He looked at Liza, who was standing off behind her brother. "You're supposed to be bad-mouthing the truck so he'll come down on the price."

"I don't need to come down on the price," Gerald said. "I always have the best price."

"That so?" Naked made a show of looking in the glove box. Empty. Not even a damn manual. "Well, let me drive her around some."

Gerald fished a set of keys from his pocket and tossed them to Naked, and then he went around and got in the passenger side. Liza went back and leaned against a white Ford F-150. Naked waved at her—maybe being cocky would piss Gerald off a little, he was such a prissy old maid—and then turned the key. The engine started right up.

"Well, what do you know?" Naked asked.

Naked put the truck in drive and pulled out of the lot onto 33/119 and headed up toward Weston.

"Rides nice," Naked said.

"It's a decent truck," Gerald said. He was looking out the window, bored, like he wasn't interested in making a sale. What a pisser.

"Liza tell you about her new job?" Naked asked. New job. Liza didn't have any job, Naked was just trying to get Gerald talking.

"No, I don't talk to Elizabeth that much," Gerald said. Like he was yawning.

Naked turned the truck around in an old lady's driveway—the poor old lady sitting up straight on her porch, looking at them hopefully, like they might be company coming for a visit—and then drove on back to the car lot. Liza was still leaning against the Ford.

"Why, it's just an old bucket of bolts," Naked said to Liza. "I think they left the best part of this truck back up in Alaska."

"I'm still not coming down on the price," Gerald said. "I don't care what you say."

"I'm just joking," Naked said. "But I am wondering what kind of deals you give Dorothy when she comes in here, you know?"

"I've never sold Mom a car," Gerald said. "So I wouldn't know."

"Oh, come on," Liza said.

"Elizabeth, stay out of this."

"You're such a liar."

"Listen," Gerald said to Naked. "You want the truck or not?"

"Gerald, tell the truth," Liza said.

"Hold on," Naked said. "You two act nice."

"I don't have to stand out here and be insulted," Gerald said. Naked saw that Gerald wasn't even looking at him—at Naked—he was looking at Liza. Gerald hated his sister bad. He looked like he was about to hit her.

"Hey," Naked said. "Over here."

Gerald blinked and turned and looked at Naked. He asked, "You want the truck or not?"

"Yeah, I guess I want it," Naked said. "Jesus."

Naked pulled out a roll of cash and made a show of counting two thousand, two hundred dollars. Gerald just stood there, watching. Naked felt like he'd been skinned, somehow. Supposed to be a big deal, buying a new truck, and here he felt skinned. Gerald standing there with his face pinched like somebody farted, like somebody dumped a bucket of shit right there in the lot.

Naked asked, "This will do it?"

Gerald took the money. He said, "I'll go draw up the papers." He walked back toward the office—didn't even invite them in for a cup of coffee.

"Damn," Naked said to Liza. "I think he skinned me on that truck."

"I wouldn't trust him," Liza said. "He's the biggest liar I know."

"He's supposed to come down a little on the price just to make me feel better," Naked said. Then he sighed. "What the hell."

Liza just shrugged. She was a pisser, too, like her brother. These Stalnakers were a tricky bunch. They all thought they were so smart.

After a while Gerald headed back from the office with a handful of paper clipped to a clipboard—the receipt, the title, temporary registration. Naked signed a few things and Gerald said, "She's all yours."

"I suppose we should go celebrate," Naked said. Buying a truck was something to celebrate, even if you got skinned on it. "Let's go for a ride."

"But what about Mom's car?" Liza asked.

"Oh, your brother can look after it for a little bit," Naked said. "Right, brother?"

Gerald looked blandly at Dorothy's Oldsmobile. He said, "I guess it'll be all right for a while." Then he turned and walked back to the office like he had a corncob stuck up his ass.

"He *guesses*?" Naked asked when Gerald was gone. "What kind of brother is he?"

"Not a very good one," Liza said. "I guess...."

Naked drove his new red truck up through Weston, down Broad Street to show it off to some people he knew—bought some pot from them, too—and then out around the old insane asylum and through some neighborhoods, honking and waving at people out working in their yards in the Saturday afternoon sunshine, and through Cox Addition, and then across the river and back downtown. A tour of Weston, and it wasn't much. Then out down 119 toward Jane Lew, and a beer joint called the Cardinal Club. Naked knew a few people there—Naked knew people everywhere—and he showed off his new truck some more, took a couple of guys for a spin up the road for a couple of miles and a couple of joints while Liza sat in the bar drinking beer, and then Naked was back and they all drank beer and played pool and the afternoon stretched on into the evening.

At some point it was later, then, much later—there was a little guy named Terry playing pool, and he only had one arm. He was good pool player, too. He'd stand up erect and line up his shot, and then hold the cue straight and steady, and pop—jab it out quick as a snake and make his shot. He was good, about as good a player as Naked sober, but Naked had been drinking and smoking all day and lost two out of the three games they played.

"Best of five," Naked said.

"That sounds right to me," one-armed Terry said. Naked squatted down and began pulling the balls out from below the table and racking them.

"How'd you lose that arm, anyhow?" Naked asked.

"Grenade went off in my hand," Terry said.

"Damn," Naked said. "Nam?"

"Oh, hell no. I never got further away than Ft. Leonard Wood. Probably saved my life, you think?"

Naked shrugged. Story of somebody's life. Somebody too fucking stupid to throw a grenade. He didn't care. Terry the one-armed guy broke the rack but didn't make anything. Naked stepped up and sank the seven ball, and then made the three ball, and then missed the five.

Naked said, "I did two tours."

And he nodded.

So there.

Terry stepped up and ran the table, made every goddamn ball just smooth and sure. He won again.

"Damn," Naked said.

"Two tours, huh?" Terry asked.

Naked held out his hand, and Liza dropped two quarters into it, for the next game. Naked said, "Go get us some beers, will you, hon?"

Liza went off to the bar. Naked squatted down to rack the balls.

"Two tours," Terry said.

"Yep," Naked said. A lie, of course. How many people did two tours of duty in Vietnam? Not very many. Naked had been in Vietnam, but he hadn't been out wading around rice paddies getting shot at. He'd been in the navy, assigned to a warehouse in Cam Ranh Bay. He'd spent most of his time in an office, a clerk, emerging in the evenings to sell stolen equipment and smoke dope and visit whorehouses. It was the best 10 months of his life, he said, and he'd tell people that the whole time he was in Vietnam he'd had flashbacks of West Virginia—he'd tell that to everybody, except the little one-armed guy in the Cardinal Club, and to that little guy he lied.

"Yep," Naked said, "I was in the shit."

The shit.

Whoever talked about being in the shit?

Liza brought over bottles of Stroh's, and one-armed Terry took one and smiled at her. She sat down at a nearby table with her own beer, and lit a cigarette. Terry smiled at her again—he had twisted rotted snaggly teeth set back in a dark beard.

"You ever think of knitting your boyfriend a shirt?" he asked. He had a few buddies clustered around the bar, and they all snickered. Naked was standing at the end of the pool table, pretending not to hear.

"You can't afford yourself a shirt?" Terry asked. "Or did you lose all your money playing pool?"

A couple of people laughed.

"Hell, I just bought a new truck," Naked said.

"Yeah? Then I expect you gave the shirt off your back for it, huh?"

More laughs.

Terry broke the balls with his little stabbing shot, made the two-ball on the break, and then the six and then missed the four. Naked missed the eleven. Terry laughed.

"Well," Naked said, "what about you? You use the same hand to jack off with and wipe your ass, too?"

"Naw, man," Terry said. "I get your mom to wipe my ass for me, and your girl, here, she plays with my pecker."

And that was it. Naked came around the table and grabbed Terry's shirt, but Terry brought his cue up and smacked Naked in the side of the head—not hard, more of a glancing blow. They tussled around the table and then the bartender was there with a baseball bat. "Take it outside!" he yelled. "Take it outside!" And everyone rushed pushed out the back door of the bar into the parking lot, graveled in places, muddy in others, dark and shadowy. "Fight!" someone yelled. "Fight!" A circle formed around Naked and one-armed Terry.

"Kill him, Naked!" Liza yelled.

Someone said to her, "You don't know nothing."

Naked rushed at the one-armed man, but Terry

scurried around and kicked Naked in the chest and knocked him back a step. People laughed.

"What?" Naked asked. "Come on, you little shit."

Naked lunged forward again, and this time Terry kicked him in the face. Naked had been in dozens of fights and beat up a lot of people over the years—he was kind of a bully, after all, it was what he did in his life—but no one had ever kicked him in the face before. Terry tried to kick him again, but this time Naked caught hold of Terry's foot and they danced around until Terry twisted away. Naked swung and missed and Terry kicked him square in the face. Just about everybody in the crowd was hooting.

"Ow," Naked said. Surprised and hurt. He felt at his nose. "Ow."

The one-armed guy stepped up then and kicked Naked in the nuts, and Naked went down on his knees, and then to his side, and then Terry started stomping on Naked.

Liza then jumped up on Terry's back and started smacking on his head—but he threw her off easily and she landed hard in the weeds, scraping her hands on the gravel or maybe on broken glass. Terry went back to stomping on Naked, and two or three of his friends joined in, somebody threw a busted concrete block down on Naked, and somebody else was pounding on him with a tree branch they found. Then somebody yelled, "This ain't fair—I'm calling the law!" Then a couple of men chased the would-be law caller off, and everyone else ran away and peeled off in their cars, and the bar door was shut and locked and the light turned off, and one-armed Terry paused to kick out one of the headlights on Naked's new truck before he disappeared too into the darkness.

Naked was a mess. He'd been stomped good—nose broke for sure, probably an arm broke and maybe some ribs. One of his ears was half hanging off. Cut all over, bruised, bloody. A bunch of men from the bar had been stomping on him. He was all muddy and bloody and about done-for.

Liza came crawling out of the weeds, bleeding too where she'd hit the ground.

"Naked?" she asked.

"You got to get me home," Naked said.

Liza helped him up and around the front of the bar, to the new truck, and she helped him up into the passenger side. Got blood all over his nice new shiny red and black vinyl seats.

"I'll get you to the emergency room, baby," Liza said. "Don't worry."

"No," Naked said. "Take me home."

Liza got behind the wheel. The seat was too far back for her to reach the pedals, and she had trouble adjusting the seat—she could only move her end of the bench. Naked was too messed-up to pull on the lever on his end. She drove back through Weston with the half-askew seat and only one headlight. Naked was leaning against the door, leaving a bloody human grease stain on the door window.

"Man, they fucked me up," Naked said after a while. "They kicked my fucking ass."

"It wasn't fair at all," Liza said. "There must've been ten of them!"

Naked didn't say anything. He just held his one unbroken hand over his face.

When they got through to the other side of town there was the hospital off on the left, and the emergency room.

Liza slowed down. She asked, "Sure you don't want me to stop here?"

"Hell, no!"

Liza kept driving. A couple of miles further and she came up at the bend in the road at Pricetown, and there was Gerald's car lot.

The car lot with Dorothy's Olds 98 parked right out in the open under a lamp.

"Hey," Liza said. "We have to get mom's car."

"No," Naked said.

"Well—"

"Just take me the hell home."

Liza drove on. But her mom needed the car in the morning, to go to church, to go to the store. Naked lived in Glenville, then. Glenville was about 15 miles from Pricetown—about 15 miles too from Burnt House. And mom needed the car.

"Mom really needs that car in the morning," Liza said.

"She can kiss my ass," Naked said.

And then Gerald's car lot—Dorothy's car—was 100 yards behind them.

Then 200 yards.

Then a quarter-mile....

Okay.

This is how it works. Sometimes you tell a story, and the story turns out to be something other than you thought it was about when you started telling it. This story was supposed to be about Naked Jackson, after all, about how he was never anything more than a small-town pot-dealer and big-feeling thug who scared a lot of people in and around Burnt House. Instead, though, as I think it through and tell it to myself, and retell it on a page, this story is really about Liza—Liza, who, for that moment at least, found herself suddenly tired of all the shit in her life.

So.

This is what happened.

Liza gripped the steering wheel tight and pulled it left across the oncoming lane—no traffic on 119 this time of night—and busted through a barbed-wire fence and across a pasture, faster, bouncing through some brush and over rocks and a couple of small trees and then *bang bang boom* into the creek. Liza ended up bleeding across the bridge of her nose—she somehow bumped the steering wheel—but she was more or less okay. Naked had bounced and bounced and flipped over and his face was down against the floormat and his feet were up in the air.

"What—what happened?" Naked asked. Whispered.

Liza opened the truck door and fell out into the creek. The shallow water was cool—cold, even. The cold moon was up there in the sky and the hills were closing around in the dark. After a moment she stood up dripping and said, "I'll go get help."

Part Four
Get Your Ass Back in West Virginia

You Starve Alone

How old was Gran then?

In 1975, when I started spending entire summers in Burnt House while my parents did whatever they were doing, she was 62. Now that I'm too rapidly approaching that age, 62 doesn't seem old at all. But she sure seemed old then. And, the thing is, she really *was* old—at 62, Gran was a worn-out broken-down old lady.

She'd had a heart attack in 1973—Dad said she loved Richard Nixon so much that Watergate about killed her. She was permanently weakened from that, I think, and she took what seemed like random handfuls of pills for her blood pressure and heart rate and who knows what-all else. She had Type II diabetes, which was essentially untreated—she took what she called "sugar pills" for it, but she never actually checked her blood sugar that I could see, and her diet was the traditional West Virginia diet, heavy on white bread and white potatoes and salt and sugar and pork. She was overweight, though not obese; a stout woman who had once been physically powerful, a hard worker who worked hard, and harder, and harder, until she eventually worked herself out, broken.

Gran was depressed. We didn't know what depression was, then, but now, from a distance, it seems obvious. It would have been hard for her not to have been depressed! Her dad was a sometime preacher and full-time drunk who beat his wife and kids with chunks of stove wood, and then she married my granddad, who was a diligent hard worker but was, by all accounts, a bit "odd-turned"—a drinker, too, and sometimes violent, a hard man to be married to. Her children—my dad, Gerald, Liza—were hard kids to parent, willful, silent, disrespectful, and too often unwilling to help her out as she aged. Her grandchildren were next to useless. On that day in 1978 when Dad complained that the house on Stalnaker Run was falling into disrepair, all he did was complain, and he was, of course, correct. But who was there to do the work for Gran? Who wanted to help her? My dad certainly didn't pull his shirt off and get to work mowing the yard or painting the porch or cleaning the gutters or doing any of the other very many jobs there were to do around the house. He just bitched around and cursed at people and made everybody feel bad, and then he went back to Ohio.

So Gran was depressed, though she wasn't morose. Life was tough but she made do. She went to church on Sundays, and when her car wasn't wrecked, she went to town once or twice a week to run errands, and she visited with her lady friends. Her life had been a hard one, for the most part, and if she was living in those years with few emotional rewards—well, then, it's been my observation that there are very few emotional rewards in this world for anyone. This is all there is.

Depressed or not, Gran was the only person in my family who was kind to me on a consistent, regular basis—which is to say, always. Always. I let her down like everyone else let her down, but in those years she gave me the only home I had. I spent some of my time living with my mom in horrible apartments in Columbus while she tried to work on her PhD, and I spent more of my time with my dad in one of the quickly formed and dissolved homes he tried to make in Toledo. By law, I was an Ohio resident, but I told people—and still tell people—I grew up in Burnt House, West Virginia. I overheard Gran tell my dad once, "This is the only real home she's ever known," and that was true.

Gran often said, "Eat and the world eats with you, starve and you starve alone." She'd known starving, I think, when she was young, hunger at least, after her mom died and her crazy drunk daddy died and she was passed around to various relatives who didn't want to have anything to do with her except beat her or abuse her. Not a lot of food for her then and even less kindness. Still—Gran was a good cook, and would, when she was feeling well, work up solid West Virginia meals featuring sausage and gravy, or pickled beans, sometimes fried green tomatoes, fried yellow squash, or my favorite, fried chicken. Sometimes she'd fry chickens twice a week for me. At the end of one summer, I bugged—begged—her to tell me how to do it, so that I could have her chicken wherever I was living then back in Ohio.

"Well, frying chicken's a lot of work," she told me.

"Sure," I said. Guessed. I was never allowed to hang around the kitchen, had never watched her cook. I didn't know anything. The food just appeared on the table—a miracle.

"Why do you want to know for?" Gran asked.

"So I can make some chicken when I get back?"

Of course.

Dad would actually cook breakfast for me every morning—he was a big breakfast man, eggs, toast, oatmeal, coffee, bacon or sausage. But the rest of the day I was pretty much on my own. And then when dad traveled, he'd be gone for two or three days at a time, and I would be wholly on my own. At least I knew how to open a can. But I wanted some of Gran's chicken.

Of course?

"Well, I don't know," Gran said. She frowned, grimaced, and looked around the kitchen, which Liza, under some duress, had sort of cleaned. "I guess. Well, what you do is, you heat you some oil in a pan—"

"A frying pan, okay," I said.

"—and dust in some seasoned flour—"

"Seasoned flour?"

"With salt and pepper or whatever you have," Gran said. "And then you put your chicken in the pan there and cook it."

Wow—it was simple!

I could do that.

I asked, "That's all?"

"You can cook chicken that way," Gran said.

Well, it made sense to me, but only because I was bone-stupid. What Gran did that day was give me the basics for making a roux—a word I don't actually remember hearing until I was in graduate school years later and took a trip to Louisiana and someone explained to me what we were eating. But a roux is what she told me to make, and I've never heard of anyone actually frying a chicken in a roux.

But you know what? I tried. I wanted that damn chicken. My dad was pretty much of a failure at being a parent, but he always believed in keeping me fed, and he always kept food in the house, and so I kept frying chickens, chicken after chicken—three, four, five times a week. And not just when I was living with my dad—I kept working at it for years. I wanted Dorothy Stalnaker's fried chicken! I wanted it!

And I never got it.

I attempted a little variation in that weird roux, adding garlic or chili powder, I tried baking it, I tried oven frying—I tried a lot of things. I worked so hard to get that chicken right, and it always sucked. It was terrible.

I finally cornered Gran and forced her to tell me how she did it. I said I had to know, no bullshit.

Gran asked, "How did I tell you to cook it before?"

I explained. Flour in the oil. Seasoning.

Chicken in the resulting goop.

Cook.

Serve.

Be sad.

"Oh," Gran said. "Well, I think you can cook chicken that way."

"Yeah," I said. "But it's not any good."

"I guess you can still *eat* it," Gran said. "I guess it doesn't go to waste."

But—I didn't just want to eat any old damn thing! Did she not see that?

"Well, how long have you been cooking it like that?" Gran asked.

"Fuck, I don't know," I said. Gran didn't like it when I cursed, but I was getting mad, and I swore on purpose, to shock her. "Years!" I said. "Eight or nine goddamn years at least!"

I think she was ignorant of how I had been living.

"It takes some practice to get it right, sometimes," Gran said.

Yeah, well, that stupid fucking roux chicken was never going to be right.

At this point talking to her I was mad, and I got mean. I got in my car and drove the 25 miles to Weston and bought two chickens at Kroger's, and drove the 25 miles back to Burnt House in the dark. I was ready to get to work on the chicken right then, but Gran said it was too late—even though she was an insomniac and wouldn't be sleeping. She put the cut-up chicken in a pan of salt water and placed it in the fridge overnight.

Dinner for us in West Virginia was at around 11:00 in the morning, and was the biggest meal of the day (supper would at around 4:00 in the afternoon, and was usually dinner leftovers). So for a chicken dinner we got to work early, and there's no doubt I was a bitch about it. Gran was really sick by then, she'd had a stroke a year or two earlier, and she was creeping around the house like a big, gray spider. She made a huge mess, using every pan in the kitchen, flinging salt and flour and cooking oil everywhere, dropping and breaking dishes—but in the end, after about three hours of misery for both of us, we had a platter of perfect chicken.

The method she used that day—the method she had used her whole life—was totally different than the weird roux method she'd told me earlier. Watching her cook, I felt confused at first, and then betrayed.

All those years I wasted—all those hundreds of chickens I fucked up.

I asked her, "So why'd you lie to me and tell me that stupid way to cook chicken?"

"I don't know," Gran said. "I guess I didn't think you really wanted to know."

"What?"

Gran slowly turned away from me, pivoting away in her walker. She said, "I didn't think you really cared."

Didn't think I really wanted to know.

Didn't think I really cared!

Chicken à la Dorothy Stalnaker

1. Cut chicken in pieces—store bought or cut it up yourself. Soak overnight in salt water. (On the cooking shows they call this "brining," but I'm using the more accurate West Virginia terminology. Soaking).

2. Next day, remove chicken from the soaking water (pour the water out the back door, the salt will keep the grass killed so you won't have to mow it) and place it in a pot with some more salted water. Bring to a boil and reduce to simmer, and cook until tender. (Tender is a value judgment: old West Virginia ladies who lost their teeth thirty or forty years earlier, for example, will want their chicken more tender than some bright-smiling strong-toothed city girl). (Also: I've found that the breast can be overdone and dry—keep an eye on it, and maybe take it out sooner than dark meat pieces).

3. Melt a half-stick or so of margarine in a cast-iron

frying pan. (Margarine! Not butter! I probably didn't have butter until I was 25 years old or so. No one we knew ever used butter). (Though actually butter would probably taste better). (Though it might also burn).
4. Roll the tender, cooked chicken in seasoned flour—more salt, and black pepper—and brown it in the frying pan until it has a nice crust.

I make Gran's chicken a couple of times a month. And maybe once every two or three months I get it right. Sort of maybe sometimes almost close to right.

What I was after—and perhaps still am after—obviously, was a spark of memory I could carry with me always and experience again and again and again and still have that memory be new. I can get close to that memory sometimes—like my cooking, I get sort of maybe sometimes *almost* close.

A few years ago I was in San Francisco for a conference of composition teachers, and there was a nice restaurant right across from the hotel, and I went there with a couple of colleagues. We started with appetizers, and I ordered the pan-fried quail on polenta, and when it came out, it was this little brown half-bird, and I broke off a leg and tasted it—and oh! I was transported. I don't know how the chef did it, but that little light brown crust on the bird took me back and back and back—across a continent, across thirty or more years, to another place and time, to another life, to the person I was then, a bad daughter, a bad granddaughter, a bad friend, to all the people gone and forgotten or gone and remembered, to stories told and untold, to the hills looming up in the night and in my mind, to all my many failures over time as a cook and a teacher and a writer and a lover and a friend and a person, to all the guilt and regret that burned in me then and burns in me still.

I mean—goddamn, right?

That was a lot to get out of a little tiny bird that

wasn't even a chicken, a terrible cliché of Proustian, madeleine-ian involuntary memory, sure. But it was real. There I was, sitting at a table with my as-yet oblivious, chattering friends, and I began crying, weeping, feeling sorry for myself and that whole lost world I'll never get back, the taste of memory. Whew.

Oh, Gran. Gran.

You thought I didn't care.

You thought I didn't want to know.

Know These Things

Gerald Stalnaker never went back much to Burnt House, his hometown, his home, even though he only lived 25 miles or so away, in Weston. It was a longer drive than it seemed. The road was dangerous and curvy, and sometimes the weather might spit out rain or snow, and there wasn't anything he wanted to do once he actually got to Burnt House, nothing to do but talk to his mother or get annoyed by his stoned kid sister, and everything always looked so shabby and run-down and depressing. Twenty-five miles: it really was longer than it seemed.

Still there came a time when Gerald wanted to drop his boy off in Burnt House one more time for a few days. Danny Bob was in his room with the door shut, and Gerald knocked on it.

Gerald asked, "You in there?"

"Yeah," the boy said.

Gerald eased the door open. D-Bob was in bed, on top of it in a nest of blankets and sheets wearing jeans and a plain white t-shirt. A thin skinny boy with his hair cropped short.

"How you doing?" Gerald asked.

"Oh, fine," D-Bob said. He was holding a book in his hand, one of those spy novels he liked. He didn't look like he was doing fine.

"Get your shoes on and let's go see your grammaw," Gerald said.

The boy looked wildly around the room—like he was trapped. He looked at the closet door, at the window. He said, "I don't feel so good."

"You can go to bed when you get there," Gerald said. "We'll get you something to eat, first. You want to go to Pizza Hut?"

"I'm not hungry."

"Well," Gerald said. "If you eat something, you'll probably feel better."

The boy just looked away and shook his head. Still, his bag was sitting there on the floor, packed.

"Just c'mon," Gerald said. He went back to the front room and got the keys to the Buick and checked around the kitchen to make sure everything was turned off, and then there came the boy down the hall—trudging, like he was tired—carrying his gym bag.

"You're travelling light, huh?" Gerald asked.

"You said it was only for a couple nights," D-Bob said.

"That's right."

In the car the boy sat quietly and they drove through town, the river flat and dirty-looking below them, and the great granite pile of the state hospital—the old insane asylum— rising behind leafless trees. Traffic clogged the narrow streets and then they were through it and on the new strip that led out to the interstate, and the Pizza Hut.

"I'm really not hungry," the boy said. He didn't want to go in.

"Better eat anyway," Gerald said. And the boy finally got out of the car and trudged along, followed Gerald in, and they sat in a booth by the front window. Gerald ordered a large pan pepperoni and two ice teas. The boy looked out the window, looked like he wished he was a million miles away. But where else could he go? There wasn't any other place than West-by-God-Virginia. No place like it, either.

"You got a whole month off from school," Gerald said. Christmas was coming, though no one he knew much felt Christmasy. "That's pretty wild, right?"

D-Bob looked around startled. He asked, "What?"

Gerald said, "I wish I had a month off."

Which was true. He wished he had two months off—he wished he had a lifetime off, a forever off.

D-Bob quickly nodded and looked out the window.

"Well," Gerald said. "Maybe you can get you a girlfriend when school comes back. That'll cheer you up."

D-Bob looked at him, scared, and didn't say anything.

Their waitress brought their food then, and Gerald cut out a slice of pizza and put it on a platter and slid it over to D-Bob. Then he got himself a piece.

"Good, huh?" Gerald asked.

The boy didn't say anything. He blew on the slice of pizza to cool it, then cut a bit and put it in his mouth like he didn't care, like it was automatic. Maybe he really wasn't hungry. He hadn't been eating much lately. Though he always had been skinny, skinny, a frail-looking little guy.

"Yeah, it's good," D-Bob finally said. He was just picking at the pizza.

"Your mom'll be back in a few days," Gerald said. Though he didn't know if that was true. Maybe she'd be back. Maybe not.

D-Bob nodded.

Gerald thought about Nancy, the boy's mother. He said, "You think men can ever understand women?"

"What?"

That got the boy's attention. He looked at Gerald like he was crazy.

Gerald asked again, "You think men can ever understand women?"

The boy shook his head, then looked away. That look for escape. He said, "No."

Gerald smiled. "Aw, I think they can. Just takes a little

practice, is all. A little work."

With Nancy it didn't even take that much work. She wasn't afraid to say what she was thinking—she was brassy like that. She was tired of him, that's all, she said, and she found somebody else. That's all. The thing was, she didn't even know about half of what was going on, what Gerald was doing when he went out at night, the things he did. Gerald didn't think it was any of that. If she'd known, Gerald thought she would have said something—sure, she would have said something about all that. But all she said was that she was tired, and that she had a boyfriend. Tired. A boyfriend. Yeah, it was different for her. It was a hard, hard thing to take. Everything was busted now and that was the truth and that was all it was. Four or five straight months of silence broken occasionally by bickering—and Gerald had to admit, he wasn't always an easy man to get along with, he did things sometimes that weren't right—and Nancy had run off to her sister's house in Charleston to think things over, whatever that meant besides seeing her boyfriend, too, who was also living down there somewhere.

And meanwhile, poor Danny Bob sitting in his room in his bed staring off into space like his world had come apart, which it had.

What were they going to do with Danny Bob?

And meanwhile on top of that—Gerald was having to go into work each day and sit in an office across the hall from the office of Nancy's father. That was a hell of a thing, too. Bob Spence owned the car dealership—and the mobile home dealership, and a real estate office. A he was a mean son of a bitch, too. Old Bob was a skinny frowning bald man who kept his office door open and spent a lot of time squinting across the hall at Gerald when Gerald was trying to work.

There it was: wife gone, job going, son sad.

It was all a hell of a goddamn thing.

Now all there was to do was park the boy for a week

or so at Burnt House while he straightened or didn't straighten out things with Nancy, and then with her father. But he'd be goddamned if he'd take the boy to Old Bob's house and leave him there to have goddamn Bob fill his head with hate and lies. Burnt House was a pain in the ass and depressing but at least it was safe.

Now, though. D-Bob had stopped eating.

Gerald said, "I'm going to go talk to your mom."

"I know."

The boy knew nothing, really.

Gerald said, "You better eat a little more."

"Really, I'm full," D-Bob said.

"You'll be hungry later."

"No, I won't."

"You don't know what your grammaw'll have to eat out there."

The boy shrugged, looked out the window.

Well, have it your way, then, Gerald thought. Nobody takes what I say seriously, not even my own goddamn boy. Gerald waved for the waitress and told her to box up the pizza, and then he just sat with the boy in the booth. D-Bob was staring out the window, and Gerald was staring at D-Bob. What the hell was wrong with that boy? No telling. The waitress came back with the boxed pizza and the check, and Gerald slid out of the booth and stood up.

"You want to carry this?" Gerald asked D-Bob.

"Yeah," D-Bob said. Sighed. "Okay."

The boy picked up the box like it was a sack of concrete, like it was a load, like it was a burden, like it was too much to carry. Too much. That boy. A lot of things in life were too much to carry, but a pizza wasn't one of them. Gerald paid for the meal and then they were outside. D-Bob stood by the car with his shoulders hunched over holding the heavy box, not knowing what to do with it, frowning.

"Jesus Christ," Gerald said, and he snatched the box

from D-Bob and tossed it in the back seat. "Get in the damn car."

The boy didn't say anything and got in the car. Gerald pulled out of the parking lot and headed back across town. The boy was silent. Crossing the river on Second Street, he was looking down into the water.

Gerald asked, "So, what're you thinking?"

"What?" D-Bob asked. "Oh—nothing."

"You're thinking about nothing?" Gerald tried to smile. Tried to joke. "Really? That's pretty hard to do. Go on—try thinking about nothing."

The boy didn't say anything, he only blinked a couple of times and stared straight ahead. He didn't look like he was thinking about nothing.

Well, fuck me, Gerald thought. I tried.

They drove on through town and out of town, and they came up on the car dealership, and Old Bob's goddamn gray Cadillac parked out by the side, and he knew Bob was in there sitting in his office, plotting. Up to something. Bob Spence was one man you could never trust, though he built his whole life on being kindly and friendly and trustworthy. Couldn't trust him at all, though. The Spence's had been selling cars ever since there were cars made to sell, and selling horses before that back to Civil War days, a hundred and fifty years or more ago, and they knew all the tricks, they knew how to make things work out right. For them. Man, everybody thought he'd done well marrying Nancy Spence, but really it was like getting locked into some kind of slavery thing, not quite slavery but almost. Peonage. Indentured servitude. Chain gang. Prison. They paid for everything and you owed them everything, and they owned you. And it wasn't that Nancy was bossy all the time—though she was bossy a lot of the time, most of the time—it was that there were expectations when you were in with the Spence's, you had to sell cars, for one thing, but you had to bow down before Bob, too—Old Bob, God Bob—and most of all you had to be clever all the time, be devious and friendly at the same time, calculating and kindly, you had to be up to something all the time, you had to be a fake, a phony, a liar. And if you weren't—if you were as just as open and honest and straightforward as you could be about your life without telling everything that people had no right to know—well, then they just thought you were a goddamn fool, and they stepped on you. And then they laughed at you, too. The Spences. A lot of the time Gerald never wanted to talk to them, not talk to Old God Bob at work, not talk to Nancy at home, not talk to anybody—and, damn, sitting there in the car driving out Route 33, Gerald felt his own silence filling the car, and Danny Bob's silence, too, and he thought, Goddamn it, he is my own son that way. Silent.

But still he needs to talk to me.

They drove past a stretch of new fence where Elizabeth drove that truck, Naked Jackson's truck, across the meadow and into the creek. That was pretty funny, though Elizabeth always was a disappointment. An embarrassment, too—all that dope and drugs and sleeping around all the time. It was time she got married and moved away.

"Going to go see your Aunt Elizabeth," Gerald said.

"Yeah," D-Bob said. He sounded a bit happier about that, though. He liked her, for some reason.

They drove on past an old man raking leaves, blustery winter coming on, squirrel season pretty much over, and now it was deer season. Gerald hadn't been hunting for years, maybe it would be good to go out and sit in the woods and be quiet for a while. Maybe take the boy. Hell, he liked being quiet anyway.

They passed a dead possum by the side of the road.

"Hey!" Gerald said. "What's that dead possum doing by the side of the road?"

"Huh?" D-Bob looked around confused. "What?"

"What's that dead possum—back there—what's it

doing by the road?" Gerald's sudden idea was to make a joke, something like the chicken that crossed the road joke, that sort of thing. Why'd the chicken cross the road? What's that dead possum doing by the road? It was a goddamn *joke*.

"What?" Now the boy sound irritated.

"Because it's already dead," Gerald said. Which didn't even make any sense, really.

"What?"

It was no goddamn use. The boy was being stupid, Nancy was being a bitch, and Old God Bob was being a crook. Then they'd get to Burnt House and Mom would make him feel guilty about everything, and Elizabeth would be drunk or on drugs.

What a—what a fucked-up life. Wasted.

They drove silently through the little community of Pickle Street, and then veered off onto Rt. 47 at Linn. Then Troy, getting close to home, across Cove Creek, and then up Bloody Run. The boy had been watching the countryside roll by, just sitting there, looking. Gerald finally felt like he had to say something.

"Your mom and me are probably going to get a divorce," Gerald said.

"Yeah," D-Bob said. It wasn't a question. Just an acknowledgment.

Gerald slowed the car to make a tight turn going up the hill, then hit the gas coming out of it.

"I know it's rough," Gerald said, and he glanced over at the boy and then back at the road. "But your mom and me—we—we still love you and all."

"Yeah," D-Bob said. "Okay."

Then around another curve. The boy usually loved this hill—it was his favorite hill—but now he just sat silently, leaning into the curves.

"I know it's rough for you, Danny. But you need to know these things."

They drove over the top of the hill then. Sometimes

in the past, driving in with Nancy and D-Bob, or taking Elizabeth for a drive when she was young, or just by himself coming home, having fun, Gerald would shift his car into neutral and coast down the big long hill just to see how far gravity could take him—rolling free and easy, one time all the way into Burnt House itself, to Butchie's store. But this time, with his quiet, sad son sitting there, Gerald didn't feel like coasting. It didn't seem like gravity was working anymore.

Screen Door *BAM-Ba-Bam*

Gran got too sick to stay alone. She'd had a stroke in 1985 that limited her mobility, and she was also showing more and more signs of Alzheimer's—though at that point, in 1987, nobody had really heard of Alzheimer's and people would hush their voices and whisper that she was *out of her head*. She moved in with Gerald and his new wife, Sharon, though that didn't last too long, they couldn't take care of her, they didn't have the time, and so they moved Gran into an old folk's home just down below Weston.

The old house up Stalnaker Run in Burnt House hadn't been sold yet, and so that summer I had a few weeks before I was supposed to report for grad school in Missouri, and I came back and lived at home for a while. I'm not sure why. Or maybe I am sure.

Yeah, of course I'm sure.

Burnt House was different. Gran was gone, and Liza was married again and gone. Pap Talbot had moved in with Aunt Irene in Minneapolis, and that winter would later die—the house in the meantime rented out to a strange creepy old man from Boone County who would stare at me flatly and dully, almost drooling whenever I went by. Butchie was down with cancer and would later die, and

Claudie was running the store, poorly. Bess still ran the post office, and Page still ran his store, and I would stop by every day, about, to get my mail and then get some gossip, but Burnt House was different—it was quiet and unsettling. For the first time ever, I was a little lonely.

Our house on Stalnaker Run was still sturdy enough, though it badly needed painting, and the yard was a mess. All grown up. Inside, most of Gran's belonging and furniture had been picked over and carried off by Dad and Gerald and Liza, but there was some furniture of no value left, and some pots and pans, and I moved an old couch out on the porch—the swing and the glider had disappeared—and I sat out there and read in the afternoons, and in the evenings I watched the fireflies spark and the fog drift down off the hilltops.

Once when I was an undergraduate I took a creative writing class, and one day the teacher gave us a prompt for an in-class writing exercise: write about someplace important. Which was a pretty vague prompt, if you know anything about teaching writing, and only caused the students to come up with pretty vague bits of prose after their seven minutes of writing—they wrote about obvious things like hometowns and high schools. One boy wrote about a bar he liked, and a barmaid he liked, and a special pinball machine, and he made it sound funny and cute.

I wrote about Burnt House—the hometown, obviously, but I narrowed it down to our house, and the front porch. The class reaction was not positive—remember, I was attending Ohio University, and West Virginia and West Virginians were always the object of rude jokes in Ohio. We were hillbillies, always. Toothless grimy butt-rapists. One kid in the class asked if Gran smoked a pipe, and somebody else said I'd written just another old hillbilly lady sitting on a porch story, and the professor, who was from New Jersey, of all places, said I was trending toward the cliché, that I needed to be more careful in my depiction of place.

Okay, listen.

Clichés become clichés through overuse, and they are overused because they are useful, or because they represent what is assumed to be a truth. And the truth is this: people in Burnt House had porches on their houses. And people sat on those porches in the evenings.

You want to call that a cliché?

I say this: fuck you.

Go read a different book.

Our house had two porches, front and back, that ran the width of the house. If you were standing in the front yard facing the house, there was a porch swing hanging from chains on the right end, and the swing was padded with big cushions and old blankets. Then, under the front window, was the glider, a sort of couch-like piece of furniture suspended on springs. Then there was the door, and then on the left end of the porch there were a couple of wooden chairs. A very comfortable place to sit, read, talk, think, look.

There was a screen door on the porch, and the door had a spring on it to yank it shut after people passed through, and the sound of that screen door shutting—*BAM-ba-bam*—echoed always through the house, and echoes now down through the years. When I was little, somebody tied a length of black yarn to the door handle and let it dangle down, and I could pull on the yarn and yank the door open—and I'd dash through and the door would slap shut behind me *BAM-ba-bam*.

Always *BAM-ba-bam*.

Anyway: the summer that I stayed alone in Burnt House, in 1987, the screen door with its dangling black yarn was about the only thing that had stayed the same.

I only went in to see Gran once. That was enough for me, and it didn't make any difference to her. She—or what was left of her—was stashed away in a rambling old house not far from the river, and I walked in and there was a big fat woman with a helmet of black hair and a faint moustache sitting back reading *Good Housekeeping*. Then I caught the smell coming up from the house, the stench—age, shit, death, bleach. I expected that, sort of. This is how people age and die in our country, most people. The fat woman looked up at me from her magazine, and I told her I wanted to see Dorothy Stalnaker.

"In there." The fat woman pointed and went back to her reading.

In the next room, the living room, I guess, of the old house, there were seven old ladies sitting in wheelchairs. There was a TV turned to *Days of Our Lives*, but only two ladies were in a position to look at the screen; the other five were facing seemingly random directions. One old lady noticed me standing in the door and she smiled at me, but she wasn't Gran. It took me a moment to figure out which one was her—they were all so old and white-haired and shrunken. But then I recognized Gran sitting off by herself, all twisted around in her chair, staring attentively at—nothing, I guessed. I went over and pulled up a stool and sat down.

"Hi, Gran!" I said.

She looked at me—and recognized me. She said, "Jean!"

Jean was my mother's name.

"No, Gran, it's me—Jackie."

"Jean, I'm glad to see you."

"No!" I raised my voice, like that would get through to her. "Jackie!"

"Where's Bill?" My dad.

"I'm Jackie, Gran."

The old lady who had smiled at me slowly wheeled her chair over.

"Well, Dorothy," the old lady said. "You sure have a pretty daughter."

"Granddaughter," I said.

"Jean," Gran said.

"My name's Jackie," I said.

"She might know you on some better days," the old lady said.

"Jean." Gran looked from the old lady to me and then lost focus and stared past me in surprise—almost in horror, I'd say.

I just sat there. I'd heard Gran was in bad shape, but what did I expect? I had hoped that she'd at least sort of be herself. But she wasn't. What did I expect now, sitting there—what did I want from this crazy woman? Did I want her to think I was my mom, and tell me what she thought about Mom kicking Dad out and leaving me behind? Like I said, I sort of suspected that Gran didn't like my mother very well, and she probably had some good stories to tell about all that. So did I expect her side of the family dirt to come out right then? For a moment, a flash, I sort of did. But did I also want her to come to her senses and recognize me and tell me that she loved me and valued me? (Though of course she wouldn't do that in her right mind, not in a million years. People in our families didn't ever talk like that, ever.) Yeah, I wanted that, too. I guess I wanted both those things, all those things, and, of course, I didn't get them, and I never would. I just sat there waiting while Gran stared past me.

"I'm staying at the house," I said finally. "I've got the yard looking pretty good."

A lie, but she'd never know.

"I bet it does look good," the other old lady said. She was lonely, wanted someone to talk to. "I bet you all had a fine house."

"I'm moving to Missouri next month," I said. "But I'll be back to visit."

"You'll have a good life in Missouri," the old lady said. "I've been to St. Louis. Do you have a boyfriend?"

"Uh, no," I said.

"Well, you have time."

Gran kept staring past me—not just staring blankly, she was looking at something. I looked over my shoulder.

There was just a bad painting—a print—of a harbor scene.

"You looking at that picture, Gran?" I asked.

"I'm looking at those—creatures," Gran said.

"Creatures?" I looked around for a dog or a cat. A fishtank. Saw nothing.

"They're all flying around the room with air coming out their butts."

"Oh." I looked at the other old lady. She shook her head.

"She sees things sometimes. I guess we all do, sometimes."

"They're just flying around!" Gran said. "I wish they'd stop that."

Creatures. With air coming out their butts. I had to get out of there. I stood up. I said, "Gran, I have to go. I'll be back in a day or so."

I was lying again. I bet the other old lady knew I was lying, too. Maybe even Gran, all crazy out of her mind and demented and Alzheimered-up and doped on whatever kinds of heavy-duty meds they were giving her—maybe even she knew I was lying.

"Jean," Gran said. She reached out and tried to grab my wrist but I pulled away. "Don't leave me here—take me with you!"

I stopped at the Kroger on the way home, and I bought chicken and potatoes and beer, and when I got back to Burnt House I fried the potatoes and tried to make Dorothy Stalnaker chicken; and I failed. It was a total fucking mess. I ate the burned sloppy chicken anyway, though. I sat out on the porch and ate and drank and watched the evening come. A rabbit hopped out of the brush behind the cellar house and nosed around and then hopped back into the weeds. I'd meant to clear all that away, to make the house look nice again one more time, but I hadn't, and wouldn't. I remembered sitting out there on the roof of the cellar house once with Liza and smoking dope and listening to the night sounds and she was telling me about reincarnation. She was always interested in the occult—witchcraft, prophecies, Earth changes, UFOs, ghosts, the Mothman. Reincarnation, too, and she was a big fan of group reincarnation, where collections of kindred souls get incarnated together over and over and over through the ages, working out their problems over time. She believed that we chose to come back together, that we chose to live together, forever.

"It makes total sense," Liza said. "You know? We keep working together to become one with God's love."

"Oh, come on," I said.

"I'm serious!" Liza said. "Your soul made a choice to be here!"

I thought of my life—of Mom, Dad, everyone I knew in Burnt House, everyone I knew in school, everyone I ever knew, all the bullies and tyrants and fools. My God, if she was right....

"Well," I said, "I guess my soul made a mistake."

Now, years later, I sat out on the porch, positive—dead certain—that I'd made a big fucking mistake. All the weight everyone had put on me that I never wanted. Why did I choose these people to live with? My soul was out of its eternal mind. I needed to be alone forever. After a while I got up and went inside to go to bed, and I let the screen door slam shut behind me.

BAM-ba-bam.

Love Puzzle

Elizabeth was mad at her boyfriend again, her new boyfriend, whoever he was. Dorothy could never keep them straight—it seemed like they were all named John or Jack or something like that, a confusing bunch of men with long hair and rotted teeth and scraggly ugly beards. But Elizabeth was mad at whoever her man was now, and she was housebound with no way to get to town, and so she spent her evenings working on jigsaw puzzles with Danny Bob, with occasional trips out to the cellar to smoke her marijuana. Dorothy tried to ignore the two of them and watch TV, but it was a small house, and Dorothy could hear Elizabeth and D-Bob talking, and there was no getting away from them.

Dorothy was worried about that Danny Bob. Gerald had been bringing him out to Burnt House every weekend from October on, and now he was here for the whole month of December, and he was quiet and skinny and sad, and Dorothy didn't think there was much she could do for him but urge him to eat.

"Go eat some of that cake from last night," Dorothy would say. "Get in there and fix yourself a hamburger."

"I'm not hungry," Danny would say. "Really." But Dorothy saw him eat a bit of Elizabeth's cake from time to time, and once he ate all three drumsticks from a three-legged chicken she fried one day.

It was always a sad house with young people in it, Dorothy thought. Especially when the young people were sad because their boyfriends or girlfriends were treating them bad, or because their parents were treating them bad or going crazy and running off. But there wasn't ever any real happiness in life.

Since it was Christmastime, or was supposed to be, the puzzle Elizabeth and D-Bob were working on was a nativity scene, an old Renaissance painting of Mary and the baby Jesus. But it was coming together slowly. One dark late afternoon, Elizabeth and Danny were laboring over the puzzle and Dorothy came back from the bathroom and leaned on the table for a moment, resting. It seemed like puzzles were just like everything else in the world—lots of hard work for nothing.

"I don't see how you do it," Dorothy said. "Or even why you do it."

"I expect you wouldn't," Elizabeth said. "It's a puzzle."

Dorothy sank into a chair and watched them puzzle. Nothing on the TV, just cartoons and advertisements for Christmas specials. Dorothy didn't like that much—she didn't like the cartoons, but she'd always especially hated the holiday, Christmas, when kids would be home from school, and there would be extra cooking and cleaning, and wrapping presents, and worrying about money, and arguing. Fun maybe for everybody else but her. This year Elizabeth didn't seem to care too much about Christmas, either, she was mad at almost everybody, all she'd done to decorate was dig a single red glass ball out of the closet and hang it from a scrawny little Norfolk pine potted plant someone had given them. Elizabeth said, "There, that's our Christmas tree," and she sounded mad, like it was supposed to be something to be ashamed of, the little tree. But Dorothy just felt, well, the little scrawny tree was just fine. Maybe even too much. That was going to be

Christmas for them, just that little tree.

"Christmas is just another day with no mail," Dorothy said. Nobody asked her, but it was what she thought.

"Your granny's always hated Christmas," Elizabeth said to Danny.

"That's right," Dorothy said. She picked up a piece of puzzle and looked at it—a piece of background, she thought, dark-brown black, a piece of the shadowy manger—then set it back on the table. "You're too young to remember your daddy drunk on Christmas Day, waving his Barlow knife around and stabbing the packages open, and me just sitting there worrying about that turkey burning in the oven with its legs a-sticking up in the air. Some fun that was."

Elizabeth said, "It wasn't that bad."

"Yes, it was," Dorothy said. "You don't remember. Your daddy was a bad drinker. If men could just see how stupid they look drunk, they'd never drink."

Elizabeth tried fitting a piece of puzzle into Mary's head. "Maybe I'll get you a movie camera for Christmas," she said. She didn't look up. The puzzle piece wouldn't fit. Elizabeth tossed it back on the table and picked up another piece.

"I don't need a movie camera, now," Dorothy said. "But I bet you will."

"Well, I *like* Christmas," Danny Bob said.

Dorothy looked at him in surprise. "Well," she said, "I expect you do." Poor little feller, dropped off on his own, momma and daddy off somewhere wife-swapping or whatever it was they did, fighting maybe, getting a divorce, drinking, who knew where they were or what they were doing, or why. Danny did like Christmas, of course he did, and he wasn't going to have much of one this year. Dorothy thought for a moment, looked at the skinny boy, then said, "Well, I guess we can maybe go to town and shop a little and look at the lights."

Elizabeth paused, a piece of puzzle in her hand.

"You're kidding, right?"

"I don't want to stay out too late," Dorothy said. "Those roads might get slick."

Dorothy didn't have to do much to get ready—coat, keys, purse—but Elizabeth disappeared out to the cellar for a few minutes, and then shut herself in her room for hair and makeup. Danny Bob sat back in the front room and slouched down in front of the TV. Going to Weston wasn't a big deal for him—he lived in Weston, after all—but it would be good for him to get out of the house for a little bit.

Elizabeth came out eventually, looking nice, though her eyes were kind of misty, and they went out and got in the car, and Dorothy backed it out of the garage and drove down Horn Creek. The first house they came to, Hazlit's, was all lit up with red and blue Christmas lights.

"Well, they sure have the Christmas spirit this year," Elizabeth said.

"They'll have an electric bill, too," Dorothy said.

Elizabeth pointed out every house that they passed that was lit up, and most of them were lit up, it was that time of year. Finally Dorothy got tired of hearing about lights, and she said, "Elizabeth, if you like lights so much, you can buy some and put them up yourself."

"Well, maybe I will," Elizabeth said.

"And I thought you didn't want a Christmas this year."

"I don't," Elizabeth said. "Everybody's being mean to me. But I still like the lights."

"Well, get some, then."

"Maybe I will."

Though she wouldn't, of course—buying lights would cost too much money, and putting them up would take too much work.

"Oh, I'd sure like to see you out there putting those lights up on the house," Dorothy said. "You could spread Christmas cheer everywhere."

"Yeah!" Danny Bob said from the back seat.

"And you'd make Danny happy, too," Dorothy said.

"You all are too much," Elizabeth said.

In Troy almost all the houses were lit up, and even the post office had a little wreath of lights on the door. One house was dark, though—old Doc Renner, the veterinarian, who'd had a stroke.

"They took him all the way to the hospital in Morgantown," Dorothy said.

"I heard they had a time getting into his house because of those dogs," Elizabeth said. "I heard that deputy wanted to shoot the dogs, but the ambulance guy managed to get past them, somehow."

"Why'd he want to shoot the dogs?" Danny Bob asked.

"Oh, they're mean dogs," Dorothy said. "Big dogs— wolfhounds? Mastiffs? Great big mean dogs."

"He found those dogs in the creek," Elizabeth said. "During a flood. They were just puppies, and somebody threw them there in the creek to get rid of them."

"Aww," Danny Bob said.

"And those dogs love Doc Renner," Dorothy said. "That's why I always say, if you want love you should get a dog, not a person."

"Oh, Mom," Elizabeth said. "What about kids?"

"Kids are a burden," Dorothy said. "And a misery. I don't know why people do it."

"Oh, Mom."

"I sure wish I could find a puppy in the creek," Danny Bob said.

The weather turned damp as they drove—a steady misty drizzle, and the air was cool—chilly, even—but not cold enough for snow. Dorothy never drove very fast, even in good weather, and she slowed down a bit more than usual now, worried about the wet roads.

"Maybe it'll snow," Danny Bob said.

"Oh, you don't want that," Dorothy said.

"Yes, I do!"

"If it snows, you're the one who'll have to shovel off

the drive," Elizabeth said.

"Sure, I will."

"You say that now," Elizabeth said. "It's not going to snow."

"Oh, let the boy wish," Dorothy said.

"Listen to you!" Elizabeth said. "You hate snow more than anybody!"

"It won't snow," Dorothy said.

They drove through and past Pickle Street, the houses of course cheerily lit, and then up a long hill, and there was a beer joint at the top, and the beer joint was wild with lights, too. Elizabeth craned around in her seat to see if anyone she knew was parked out front.

"Well, I guess even the drinkers have the Christmas spirit," Elizabeth said.

"I'm not a drinker," Dorothy said. "I've got no spirits."

"We know," Elizabeth said. "We know."

There had been a time, a long time ago, when Dorothy was first married to Vernon, that she'd had to ride their horse all the way to Auburn once a week to get the mail and do shopping, and she'd tie the horse up outside the store with the other horses, and when she'd come back out she could never tell which horse was hers—they all looked the same, all big and brown and shaggy lined up together. She hated that, not knowing which one was hers. It was embarrassing. What if she tried to get up on the wrong horse? What if a bad horse kicked her? So that year for Christmas Vernon got her a bright-red saddle blanket so she'd be able to know her own horse. Dorothy would have preferred a new horse—a white one, maybe, or a gray one—or even better, a Model A truck, but that red saddle blanket did come from Vernon's heart, and probably was the nicest present he ever got her. So she did know about the Christmas spirit.

"Don't ever get married," Dorothy said suddenly.

"What?" Elizabeth asked.

"Don't ever get married," Dorothy said. She glanced

back in the mirror at the boy. "Either of you."

"Why'd you bring that up all of a sudden?" Elizabeth asked.

"Just a warning," Dorothy said. "You all don't want to be miserable."

"What about love?"

"Love's just all made up," Dorothy said. "It's a lie, just like everything else in this world."

"Except for dogs?" Danny asked.

"Right, except for dogs," Dorothy said. "Dogs'll love you. People don't love, though, not really."

"Boy," Elizabeth said. "You're in a great mood tonight."

They passed the long stretch below the car dealership, drove by the place where Elizabeth ran that truck through the fence and into the creek, though they couldn't see the new stretch of fence in the dark. The car dealership was closed, though the front window of the office was outlined in lights.

"Where's your granddad?" Elizabeth asked Danny. "Off counting his money?"

"Elizabeth, be nice," Dorothy said.

In the back seat, Danny Bob was silent, staring impassively out the window. Still it was probably true that Old Bob was off at some rich people's resort somewhere counting his money. That mean old man ruined his daughter's and Gerald's marriage, ruined this boy's life.

"I mean that about getting married," Dorothy said. "Both of you, don't do it."

"My lord," Elizabeth said. "You're so positive."

"I should have left your daddy," Dorothy said. "I would have many times, but people didn't get divorced back then. I'd sure leave him now."

They were coming into town, passing the hospital. Traffic was picking up, and headlights glared on the windows.

Elizabeth laughed. "But, Mom, then you wouldn't have had me!"

"You were a mistake," Dorothy said. She came to a stop behind someone who was making a left turn onto Broad Street, then moved ahead when she could. "If abortion had been legal then, you wouldn't be here today."

"Mom!"

"I was 42 years old when I had you," Dorothy said. "I was too old—it was hard on me."

"That's a hell of a thing to say."

"It's true, though," Dorothy said. "And you'd be better off, too."

They drove on in silence, past the hot dog stand and Tucci's beer joint, the wide expanse of the old insane asylum opening up on the right. Bright Christmas lights were strung up all along the street.

Elizabeth said, finally, "That's just a hell of a thing to say."

Weaning House

The Talbot family cemetery was up on the side of a pretty steep hill, and there was a graveled road—more of a bulldozer trail, actually—cut into the side of the hill, winding up into the trees. I drove up a little way but I didn't like the look of it—doubted my Honda could make it up the hill and back down—so I reversed out the way I came in, and I parked by the old house. Then I got out of the car and walked.

The trail was recently used: I could see the tracks of trucks and heavy machines, and it looked like someone was putting a gas well in back on the hill. A recent rain had left little gullies and rivulets eroded down the slope. No way my car could have made it.

The large truck tracks went on up the hill into the woods to the gas well, but a smaller trail of gravel and grass veered off through some trees and came out at the Talbot Cemetery. A line of cedars had been planted along the edge of the graves, where the hill broke sharply down, and I stood next to the trees—big, big for cedars, they must have been planted well back in the 19th century— and looked down over the hill and saw the dark slate roof of the house down below, and my car.

The graves. There were a lot of them—the Talbots had

been a big clan, though now they are all but gone, having born many men that died young and many women who married into other families. Here there were eleven rows of graves, eight rows of older tombstones, once-dark stone that had bleached and weathered and eroded over the years, and then three short rows of plain rounded rocks, placed at regular intervals. The nameless rocks showed where they'd buried babies. Maybe Vesta's dead baby was buried there. There was no way of telling.

The biggest tombstone was right in the middle of the cemetery, a shaft with a rectangle at the top, and you'd have to look at it for a minute or so to recognize it as a carved lectern and a book. The book was a bible, of course. This was the grave of Solomon Talbot, my great-great grandfather. His favorite bible verse was supposed to have been carved into the stone bible, but now it was too weathered and acid-rained away to read. I'd done some research and already knew what it was, though. Psalm 111:3.

HIS WORK IS HONOURABLE AND GLORIOUS:
AND HIS RIGHTEOUSNESS ENDURETH FOR
EVER.

The psalm is offered as a tribute of God's creation, but I have the feeling old Solomon was claiming some of the credit, too. He was a Civil War veteran who had served three years with the Army of the Potomac, an artilleryman, who came back here to Rocky Fork, had 14 children with his first wife, who died—can you blame her? Fourteen kids!—and married another woman, who raised the ones who survived. He farmed and taught school. A lifelong Republican, of course, and he lived a long time. Going through archives I found a letter he wrote to the editor of the Weston newspaper: "I cast my first vote for Abraham Lincoln, and I shall, if I am spared, cast my next vote for Warren G. Harding." One good vote, one bad.

Maybe life balances out. Solomon cast his vote and later died, and was buried here, and his righteousness was forgotten by almost everyone, except me.

I stood there by the stone bible, looking around, soft sunlight dappling through the trees. I thought, I share genes with all these dead people. These long-forgotten dead people

Someday, I'll be forgotten, too.

Damn.

I cut back down the hill to the house following a deer trail through a thicket of prickly multiflora rose and only got tangled up a little bit. Then I made my way carefully around the house, worried about falling down a well—all my life, people had been worrying me about falling down a well. Gran, Dad, Pap Talbot—old people never stopped warning me about falling down a well. I remembered once coming here with Pap and my mom when I was eight or ten, and Pap yelling at me to stay close, "Goddamn it, Jackie, look where you're a-going! You're going to fall down a goddamn well!"

I wasn't going to fall down any goddamn well.

Then, or now. Or ever.

The house. It was a big, wooden, two-story place with all the windows long ago busted out. Inside, there was a central hall with rooms opening on either side. I stepped into the front room, all dusty with plaster coming off the walls and dirt blowing in through the broken windows. I liked the large wooden mantelpiece over the fireplace—it was solid and well-built and could probably be restored and made to look nice. How would I fit it in my car, though? And where would I put it? I didn't have a house, and was likely never to have one, and my dad was busy starting up another new home and he never much liked old things, anyway. He was a plastic man.

So, no fine old mantelpiece.

In the hallway, stairs led up to the second floor. I didn't trust them at all and didn't try them. Down at the end of the hallway was the kitchen, and I peeked in there: utter ruin, with one grotesque oddity—a fleshy pink fat doll baby face down in the dirt, next to an overturned table. Missing an arm. Creepy.

Back outside I stood on the steps. In old photos, the house has a narrow, two-story porch at the front. In one, taken on the occasion of a Talbot family reunion, Solomon and his second wife—her name was Thelma—are sitting in chairs, formally dressed, on either side of the door. In another photo they are standing out in front of the house, and the house itself is surrounded by a throng—all the living children and grandchildren and greats and all their husbands and wives—a vast army of family.

But now the porch was gone. Someone had pulled it down, for some reason. Now there were just a few cracked cinder blocks stacked up out front for steps. I stood there and looked around—and saw a big patch of jonquils growing at the corner of the house. Jonquil: Liza named her oldest daughter Jonquil, a silly name for a human but a pretty flower nonetheless. I went and got a spade from the back of my car—Pap Talbot, of course, taught me to keep tools in my car always—and I dug up a big clump of the flowers. They came easily from the dry soil and I wrapped the roots in an old towel and put them on the floor of the backseat.

I remember one time when I was fairly little and looking through a box of old photos taken at that reunion. I gazed for a long time at a picture of Solomon's daughters and granddaughters, and there was Aunt Vesta sitting there in the middle, young and determined and staring out at the world so angrily that I'm surprised the camera didn't melt. After a while I moved past it and on to the other pictures, wondering, asking questions, curious about the old, gone people, and Grammaw Talbot said, "Well, I guess Jackie's going to be the family historian." And, you know, I was proud of that, and happy, and I felt that I belonged, that I had value. But how stupid was I when I was young? Years and years later I thought about what she'd said, about family history, and my role, and I came to believe that history and memory were burdens. For years I was the one who had to know everything. I was the one who *did* know almost everything. But knowing never did me any good. Even that day, standing there outside the old Talbot house, down the hill from the Talbot cemetery, even that day history and memory sure seemed like burdens. I could feel all those generations of Talbots, the ancestors, those forgotten selfish ghosts, floating around, staring at me, whispering "Remember me! Remember me!" And there were far too too many of them to know, or care about, or remember—and they were all dead. Dead! Most of them were probably nice enough people when they were alive, and they probably didn't deserve to be forgotten when they were dead, buried down in the stony red dirt beneath tombstones with the names eroded away so that you couldn't even tell who was buried where—and those dead babies, too, buried down in the dirt beneath their bare, nameless rocks. But they all were forgotten now and dead and I had no idea who they were, and I didn't want their burdens. As it was, I had living people to remember, too many of them, and they were more than burden enough. Memory itself was a burden. People were a burden. Life was a burden.

I got in my car and drove down the road, slowly. Just around the bend there was a log cabin, half-collapsed and run-down and overgrown, set back among the trees. This was Solomon's first home when he got back from the war, before he built the big house. Later, as the family grew, and he and Thelma were living up the road in the big house, his children would marry off and set up housekeeping in the old cabin, for a while, to get used to being on their own. They called it the weaning house.

I didn't get out of the car. Just sat looking out the open passenger-side window. I wanted a weaning house of my own. But then I guessed the old Stalnaker house off

Horn Creek was my weaning house, sort of.

Maybe I didn't have anything to bitch about.

Down the road a bit more was the schoolhouse Solomon built, and it was in very good condition—a subscription went around to all descendants of the Rocky Fork families to pay for its upkeep, and reunions were held there every summer. A simple frame building, painted white. I got out of the car and peered in a window or two—folding chairs, a card table, nothing much interesting that I could see. I took some pictures and got back in the car.

I sat there for a moment, feeling low.

Well. So much for Rocky Fork.

So much for the Old Country.

The weaning house.

I started the car and drove on down the road and came out on Route 5 just above Gilmer Station, and then I drove along the Little Kanawha River back to Glenville, and up through Alice, and back to Burnt House.

At home I separated the jonquils out into two bunches and I planted them on either side of the back porch steps, and gave them a good watering. The next morning, though, I looked out at those flowers while I made my coffee, and they made me sad: Dad and Gerald were going to sell the house soon enough, and I was never going to see those flowers bloom.

GTO

Here's a joke that was popular when I was a kid:

> Q: What's the most popular car in West Virginia?
> A: It's a GTO...going...to...Ohio!

Ha-ha, right?

It's a joke that works because it represents the truth. People leave West Virginia all the time, very often to Ohio, to find work, to make better lives. My dad left, my mom left, and it was my time to leave, too. I was going to be one of those people who came home only for funerals—and, then, after everyone died, I'd never come home.

And so, there I was, on my very last day in Burnt House, slouched down out on the front porch with my feet up on the banister, when I heard a car coming up the creek, and it came up around the brush and the collapsed barn and pulled up into the yard, an old, blue, rusted-out Chevy Nova with a big dent in the side. Liza. She waved at me and parked beside my car.

I stood up and watched Liza get out of the car and then lean into the backseat and pull out a daughter, a toddler named Glady-Lee. Another little girl of five or so—Jonquil—got out of the car on her own and disappeared

"

around the back of the house. Liza hefted Glady-Lee onto her hip and came on over.

"Well, look at you," Liza said.

Look at Liza: she was heavier—two kids, I guess, can do that to you—with a saggy, sort of pooched-out belly. She was missing a tooth—whether from a car wreck, a boyfriend's fist, or bad West Virginia dentistry, I don't know.

"Hey!" I said. Liza came up the steps and we hugged, Glady-Lee drooling, and then Jonquil came tearing through the house, coming in through the back and bursting out the front, the door slapping shut behind her, *BAM-ba-bam.*

The little rat. *BAM-ba-bam.* That was my sound.

But I tried to remember my manners. I smiled.

"Momma, the TV here's tiny!" Jonquil said.

Which was true. All I had was a little black and white portable my dad got me for Christmas one year. I was certainly TV deficient back then.

"We didn't come here to watch TV," Liza said.

"Then why'd we come here?" Jonquil asked.

"To visit your cousin Jackie," Liza said.

"Hi, there!" I tried to be cheery, though I knew I was affecting that horrid adult phoniness I hated so much as a kid. Oh well.

Jonquil knew I was a phony. She looked at me mistrustfully—maybe a bit angrily, evilly, too—and half-hid behind her mother.

"She's just shy," Liza said.

I doubted that.

I said, "Let's go inside—I'll get dinner up for you."

I was trying to offer Dorothy Stalnaker hospitality. One last time. Trying. Look at me, how hospitable I was: I fried up a chicken, which turned out okay though not quite right, and I had cornbread from a mix, and mashed potatoes from a mix, and ice tea from a mix. It was all pretty mediocre, but Liza was impressed at the trouble

I'd taken, and she seemed to enjoy the food. Jonquil took a bite or two off a thigh and turned up her little nose at the rest. Glady-Lee made a mess. I tried not to look at the children.

It was almost dark by the time we finished—a late supper—and Liza surprised me by actually helping to clear off the table and dump the dishes in the sink, where they stayed forever, as far as I know. I'd bought a chocolate pie at Kroger's, and I brought that out and served it up, and I also had a big jug of red wine.

We sat out on the porch with the jug, while the girls sat inside on the sagging couch with pie, watching *TV's Bloopers and Practical Jokes*.

I poured a coffee mug of wine, and I said, "I remember Gran telling me about back when Granddad was drinking, how she had to go to the state store to get his whiskey, and she was coming out of the store and she dropped a bottle and it broke. She said she was so embarrassed— the whiskey running everywhere on the street and people seeing it, thinking she might be a drinker."

Liza shrugged. "People say bad things about Daddy, but he wasn't that big of a drinker."

That's not what I heard, ever. But of course I wasn't there. Who knows?

I said, "Yeah."

"He was funny," Liza said. "I remember they'd all play cards, and he'd laugh and laugh."

Maybe they were drinking and playing cards at the same time. But, again, I wasn't there. All I'd ever heard was stories.

In the end that's pretty much all there was to my life, stories, and more stories.

I guess that's all there is to anybody's life. Everybody's life. All of us.

Liza said, "One time there was a big snow, a blizzard, and it was early, at Thanksgiving, and I went out and I was playing in the snow, right down there in the yard by the creek, and Mom came out here on the porch and started fussing at me, telling me to get back inside, that I was going to get wet, that I was going to get sick, and Daddy said, 'Leave her the hell alone, Dot, she'll never see another snow like this again,' and I never did."

So there. I nodded for her.

I said, "Wish I'd known him."

Liza brought out a baggie of pot and a pipe, and she filled it and lit it and took a hit. She passed the pipe over to me and I took a hit, too.

I exhaled. I said, "One time, Pap Talbot told me—"

"Oh, that mean old man," Liza said. "I know he's your grampaw but I hate him."

"Yeah, well," I said. "He told me he was working with Granddad once, laying a pipeline across the Ohio River, above Parkersburg somewhere—"

"They laid a lot of pipelines," Liza said.

"Yeah—"

"I mean, they all worked for the pipeline company back then."

"Yeah," I said, "I know. And—"

"They laid pipelines, it was what they did...."

"Yeah, so, they were on a boat, and it was foggy, and they were going out on the water, and the shore, West Virginia, it was disappearing into the fog, and Granddad said, 'Goodbye, ol' USA! Goodbye!'"

That story didn't come out quite right. I get high pretty easily. It was funny when Pap Talbot told it. He said Granddad Stalnaker had been drinking all night, was probably still drunk coming to work that early morning in the cold fog. I'm sure Pap Talbot hated that, he was always so serious about work. I could picture them out in that boat on the river, the known world—the old country, the homeland—disappearing into the fog, into the past, a memory. Forever, maybe. Goodbye! Goodbye! And yet they were just a couple of men doing a hard job.

Goodbye, ol' USA!

"Yeah," Liza said, "Daddy could say some funny things sometimes."

Jonquil came out onto the porch and cuddled up next to Liza on the couch.

"Bowl, momma?" Jonquil asked.

Liza filled the pipe and lit it and held it for Jonquil. Jonquil took a long hit and sank back on the couch.

I sat there watching. I remember Gran telling me about a lady she knew from church who poured a box of black pepper down her little son's throat because he cursed at her. I was shocked. I asked, "Didn't you call the police? Didn't anybody call the police?" Then Gran was shocked—she just looked at me like I was crazy. She said, "Wasn't any of our business." And so maybe this dope-smoking baby wasn't any of my business, either.

Still, I think I must have made a face or something. Liza picked up on it.

"It's good for her," Liza said. "It's natural, it doesn't do any harm, it keeps her quiet."

"I guess," I said. I knew a boy in college who had a dope-smoking toy poodle. The little white dog would cuddle up next to him like Jonquil cuddled next to Liza, and he'd be all shivery and expectant, and then my friend would hold the dog close and blow pot smoke into his face. The little dog would stagger and fall over twitchy and happy, and after a few moments would jump up and want some more smoke. Just about everybody laughed— and, yeah, I laughed, too.

Jonquil held the pipe out again, and Liza lit it for her. Jonquil sighed, stoned and content.

"Jonnie's a little party girl," Liza said. She hugged Jonquil, who was all limp and floppy. "Right, baby?"

Jonquil gazed around, stoned. I was stoned, too. Evening came, mist crept down the hillsides. Lightning bugs sparked. Liza got hungry again and stomped back to the kitchen, and Jonquil wobbly followed her. I sat a while longer, listening to the night sounds, and then I was hungry, too, and I got up and went inside.

Glady-Lee was sitting at the table making another mess, squashing up the last of the melting pie, and Liza and Jonquil were making a mess in the kitchen. Liza had found boxes of old cake mix, a chocolate cake and a strawberry cake, and she was combining them to make one giant weird cake, just like we used to do. Jonquil noticed me sitting at the table, and she tugged on Liza's shirt and pointed at me.

"Momma, look."

Liza looked at me, too, and patted Jonquil on the head. "That's Jackie, honey. She's supposed to be here. She lives here. She's supposed to be here."

Right. I was supposed to be here. Right? I poured myself another mug of wine. Liza was pouring the cake batter into flat pans.

"I broke up with John Two," Liza said. "I kicked his ass right out, after the way he acted."

John Two was John Waugh, her third husband— though I guess by that time, he wasn't. John One was John Morrison, Jonquil's father. Glady-Lee's father was Earl something-or-other, a mystery man I never met.

Liza said, "I couldn't take his shit any more. He was always going off—one time he went off to do the laundry and didn't come back for six weeks."

I asked, "What'd you do for clean clothes?"

"Didn't have any explanation when he got back, either," Liza said. "You'd at least think he could come up with a good story."

"Good stories are important," I said.

"Yeah, but I don't have time to listen to stories," Liza said. "That's your problem—really, you spend too much time listening to stories. You need to go out and do things."

"I do things!" I said.

Liza shook her head. Not at all impressed with my things. She slid the pans into the oven and then came over and sat down at the table. She wiped pie from Glady-Lee's face—Glady-Lee had been staring around kind of stupidly with smears of chocolate on her cheeks—and then poured herself a mug of wine.

"Let's go to town," Liza said. "This place is depressing. I don't want to hang around here all night."

Before I could say anything, Jonquil popped up at Liza's elbow with the pipe and the baggie of pot.

"Bowl, momma," she said.

"You're going to have to go to bed after you eat your cake," Liza said.

"Okay, momma." Jonquil was staring at the pipe. Liza lit it and took a short hit for herself, and then held the pipe for Jonquil, and Jonquil tried to hold the smoke a long time, like the adults, but she exploded into a fit of coughing and felt her way backwards onto a chair.

"Be careful, now," Liza said.

Glady-Lee started squealing then and pointing at the pipe. Liza filled it again and then took a big hit herself, and she held it down while she fumbled with a near-empty roll of paper towels. She held the towel tube at her mouth and put the other end tight against Glady-Lee's mouth and shotgunned the smoke right into the baby.

"Aw, Liza!" I said. "She's too young for that."

As if Jonquil wasn't, and I just sat there and didn't say anything. But still.

"Just makes her sleepy, is all," Liza said. "She's a little party baby."

Both the girls were sitting there glassy-eyed. Liza hefted them into the front room and plopped them down on the couch in front of the TV. The timer in the kitchen went off. I sat there while Liza pulled the cakes out of the oven and cut pieces. She took dishes of cake to the girls, and placed a dish of cake down in front of me. Actually, after the wine and the pot, the gooey, sweet, half-baked cake kind of hit the spot. But then I was pretty loaded.

Liza sat down with her own dish of cake. She said, "Let's go to town."

"Play pool at Butchie's?" I asked. "Claudie's closing up pretty early since he got sick."

"We could go over to Glenville," Liza said. "See what's going on."

I took a breath, about to say No—

"The girls can sleep in the back of the car—they like that."

"I can't," I said. "I'm heading back to Toledo tomorrow to get my stuff out of Dad's garage, and then I have to move...."

"Well." Liza looked at me for a moment. Stared at me—high, thinking. "Well—you can stay with the girls, right? Maybe I can bring the party back here."

No. Well, like, what if Liza picked up bad habits from John Two and went off for six weeks and didn't come back? I'd be stuck with those girls. I'd soon run out of cake and weed.

"No, no—I'll be back," Liza said. "Don't worry. I just want to see what's going on."

What the hell. I had to get up in the morning. I was still getting up in the morning—I was going to get up in the morning. I was already packed. I was going.

Liza stood in the doorway to the front room. "I'm going to town for a bit," she told the girls. "You mind your cousin Jackie."

Then Liza rushed around looking for her car keys. "I won't be late," she said, and then she was gone out the back door. I heard her car start and there were flashes of light on the windows as she turned around, and then red taillights.

That was quick. Liza really did hate Burnt House. She was always looking to get away—except for the times she actually got away, and then she was looking to get back. She was never happy where she was, which sort of complicated her life.

I poured another mug of wine and then looked in on the girls. They were passed out on the couch, gray-blue from the TV light flickering on them. Good. I went out on the porch and sat out there and watched the night, and the moon almost came up over the hilltop, a glow at the rim of the tops of the trees, and I could hear deer down by the creek splashing in the water, and it was good. I thought about Liza talking about playing in the big Thanksgiving snow when she was little. It probably didn't really happen the way she told the story, but that didn't matter. I'd seen snows like that, too. I remembered one time I went for a walk in the woods at night, after a big snow. The snow fell all day quietly and softly—the day was almost windless—though the snow stopped by dark and the clouds moved on, and the sky cleared and the moon came out full, and Gran was asleep so I went out as quietly as the snow fell, and I climbed the hill behind the house in the dark, through the leafless trees and moon glinting off the snow, everything alive and still, the world as perfect and simple as it usually is only in dreams and hardly ever in waking life. I went on shuffling up the hill through the woods, and I came out in a sort of clearing where five or six good-sized trees had been felled into one another in the shape of a box, sort of—the remains of a fort my father and his brother had once tried to build out in the woods when they were boys, the trees big enough to be worth something to a logging crew but just chopped down atop one another and later forgotten and left to rot, to return to the hill, grown up and taken over by multiflora rose and blackberry vines and smaller trees pushing their way through and now all covered in powdery snow glowing from the full moon in the sky. I sat on a log and looked back the way I came—the house invisible down below, all I could see through the right of way were hills and more hills all glowing in the dark under the moon. How old was I then? Young. Fifteen? Sixteen? Old enough to feel something strong. And I *did* feel something—something sad, sadness along with the beauty of the night. All those hills out there, that moon—everything so big, and all the people and all the things people did were just—nothing. They didn't matter. Something like that. Maybe. I didn't know then, don't know now, what it was I felt. But I was feeling something sitting there on that log, and I do remember thinking about my father—how he cut this big tree down and how it was rotting away and no one will ever remember anything about it except me.

And—there. That was something. I remembered a time I fell off my bike and scraped my knee and Dad laughing as he bandaged me up. He said, "Aw, you'll never know it in a hundred years." He said that the time I fell off a swing set at school, too, and other times. You'll never know it in a hundred years. He took a long-term view.

My father, my dad—the angry man, the volcano man. A history professor at the University of Toledo, he'd come a long, long way from Burnt House. But he never forgot or let anyone else forget where he came from. I remember sometimes driving around with him, and if a car up ahead was nosing out into an intersection, Dad would say, "Get your goddamn ass back in West Virginia."

He didn't say that all the time. He didn't say it constantly. But he said it often enough to make his point. If you were playing pool and your cue ball was across the line, if you were watching a football game and a player was offside, if your car was entering an intersection, if anything of yours was ever out of place—then you or it needed to get your ass back in West Virginia.

It was clear. Seemed clear, at least. If you were from West Virginia and weren't there right now, then you needed to get your ass back. Quickly. If you were in West Virginia you needed to keep your ass there and not leave. But what about his angry ass? I always wondered about that. What was he doing spending his life teaching college in Ohio? He was just another goddamn hypocrite, I figured.

One time we were playing pool, and I asked him.

He had just racked the balls. I was about to break.

"Come on," he said. "Get your ass back—"

Before he could finish I rolled my ball back, maybe an inch. Behind the line.

"—in West Virginia."

I stood up and looked at him.

"But what about you?" I asked. "How come your ass isn't back in West Virginia?"

Dad was chalking his stick. He stopped, squinted at me for what seemed like a long time. He asked, "What do you know about my life?"

I thought for a quick moment. I knew some things, a lot of things, a lot more than he might think I knew. But I also knew to lie.

I said, "Nothing."

"That's right. You don't know anything." Dad looked at me. He was kind of pissed, but he was also kind of smiling, too. "You're a strange one, Jackie. Now, shut the hell up and break those balls."

Now, though, all that time later, years later, it was late summer and cool and misty and I was sitting on the porch of the old house and Liza was off somewhere and there were a couple of stoned children passed out inside. My ass was in West Virginia. But it didn't need to be. It wasn't going to be. I finished my wine and went back inside—stopping the screen door before it slapped shut. I went to the bathroom and took a quick shower and went steaming clean to bed and fell quickly asleep—not dreamy sleep, just soft. Nice.

I woke up when Liza came home. Heard a car—cars?—outside my window, and I woke startled, and after a moment I realized what was going on, and I got up on my elbow and peeped outside. Liza's beat up car and another—no, a pickup—too. Then heavy steps on the front porch and the screen door opened.

Liza said, "Ssshhh! They're all asleep."

A man's voice whispered, "Good!"

Someone eased the screen door shut. No slap. Heavy

tip-toeing through the front room. Then the clink of coffee mugs. Wine. Whispers, low voices. A body bumping the kitchen table. A man's laugh. Then they went into Liza's old room, which was next to mine, and the bedsprings began to *screek-screek-screek*. After a while I drifted back to sleep.

When I woke again, it was light. I felt like something was wrong. I looked up and a little angry ugly face was looking back at me.

Jonquil.

"You don't got any milk," she said.

"I don't drink—uh." My mouth was dry. Cottony. "Drink milk."

"Well, I want some." Jonquil ducked back out of the room and disappeared.

I pulled on a pair of cutoffs and went out front. Glady-Lee was sitting on the couch staring around groggily. The door to Liza's room was open—they'd left it open, or Jonquil had opened it—and I saw mostly a big mound of blankets in there, and a man's hairy shoulder. I eased the door shut.

Jonquil was sitting at the dining room table eating dry brown-pink cake and smacking her lips. I went in the kitchen and got her a glass of ice tea.

"The water here tastes funny," Jonquil said.

"It's well water," I said. "It's supposed to taste funny. It's got minerals in it."

"Well, I don't like minerals."

Everything was a mess. The house was a mess, but it was Liza's mess. I could leave it. I was leaving it. I looked around. What to do? Damn, I thought. Just, damn. Just leave. My car was already mostly packed. All that was left was a small suitcase, and my book bag, and my inadequate television.

Just leave, I thought. It's time.

And so I did. I snapped shut the suitcase and zipped my book bag and carried them out to the car. Glady-Lee watched me dully. Then I came back and unplugged the television.

"Hey," Jonquil said. "What're we going to watch?"

"I don't know," I said.

When I came back to the house, Glady-Lee was tottering into the dining room. Jonquil was cutting her a piece of cake with a greasy butcher's knife. I walked back through the house—kitchen, dining room, bathroom, front room, my room—to see if I had forgotten anything.

I didn't forget anything.

Liza's bedroom door was open again. I stuck my head in and said, "Liza, I'm taking off, now."

Her arm came up out of the blankets and waved.

"I'll come back at Christmas!"

She waved her arm.

Jonquil appeared next to me, glaring around, holding that big dirty knife in her hand like she was about to stab someone—like she was going to stab me. I pushed the knife blade away and patted her on the head.

"You take care of your sister," I said.

Then I was out the screen door—*BAM-ba-bam* one last time—and into my car. I started it and backed carefully around Liza's boyfriend's dented rusted pickup, and then I drove down Stalnaker Holler, down Horn Creek, up through Burnt House. Claudie was out in front of Butchie's store, as usual, hosing down the steps. I honked and waved and she squinted at me through her glasses. Past the schoolhouse and the church, past Gid Ellyson's house, Gid's unhappy hard-working wife, Tressie, out slowly mowing the yard at her age, past the Talbot house, the creepy renter from Boone County thankfully out of sight, the house and our old garage and barn all empty-seeming now with Pap gone, the yard a sad and ugly overgrown mess, past the post office with Bess inside sorting mail, past Page's store with Page inside gossiping. I didn't stop to see them—didn't stop to see anyone. There was nothing more I could say. Nothing more I could listen to. I took old Route 47 out of town, twisting and turning through the hills and over the hills, and at a place called Longview I could peep out through the trees while I was driving and see the green misty hills stretching away, hill after hill—and I had a flash of that same feeling I'd had years earlier, looking out at the hills that night after the snow, the vastness of the world, thinking about all those houses tucked away between the hills, all those people, all those lives, loves, it was such a big world, too big to know—and I drove on, the road curving past more houses and more lives and more stories, the stories of people I didn't know, would never know, didn't want to know—I had enough stories, already, too many—and I eventually came out just before Parkersburg, and I headed north on the interstate and crossed the Ohio River, and I rolled down my car windows to flush all the West Virginia air out of the car. Breathe new. Leave that old air behind— leave behind the old stories, I thought, and all the ghosts— and the West Virginia hills too disappearing behind me in the hot summery haze—Goodbye, ol' USA! Goodbye!

Acknowledgments

Thanks—of course!—always to all the many good writers and critics and citizens and friends who provided advice and help and encouragement with this book in all its incarnations: Andrea Bates, Patricia Bjorklund, Pamela Booton, Chris Carmona, Velicia Jerus Darquenne, Florence Davies, Ken Fontenot, Phil Gavenda, Jason Harris, Suzanne Heagy, Alysa Hayes, Larry Heinemann, Kathryn Lane, Donna Long, Jerome Loving, Janet McCann, Moon Set-Byul, Laura Leigh Morris, Skip Morris, Chuck Taylor, David Thomas, Reji Thomas, Javier Booton, Sienna Ward, Diane Wilson, Alicia Wright.

Don't forget: Mountaineers are always free.

•

Some parts of this novel have been previously published:

Texas Writes: "Sleep Enough" | *Still: The Journal:* "July 17, 1978" | *Kestrel*: "As Worthless as Anyone Else" (as "Worthless") | *Kestrel*: "Guernsey Cows" | *Chagrin River Review*: "Baby Never Grew"

Thanks, editors!

About Lowell Mick White

Lowell Mick White is the author of seven books: novels *Normal School* and *Professed* and *Burnt House* and *That Demon Life*, story collections *Long Time Ago Good* and *The Messes We Make of Our Lives*, and the creative writing text *Answers Without Questions*. His work has been published in many literary journals, including *Callaloo*, *Iron Horse Literary Review*, and *Still: The Journal*. A winner of the Dobie-Paisano Fellowship and a member of the Texas Institute of Letters, White received his PhD from Texas A&M University.

Contact Lowell Mick White at www.lowellmickwhite.com